First Thing I See

By Vi Keeland

Text Copyright © 2013 by Vi Keeland

All Rights Reserved. This book or any portion thereof may not be reproduced or used in any manner whatsoever without the express written permission of the publisher except for the use of brief quotations in a book review.

To the best looking man in the class of '89. Thank you for keeping the kids out of the room while I typed my mommy porn. And for not thinking that I am anymore insane for doing this.

Chapter 1

Today, I start over. Hope stared in the mirror trying to convince herself that today would be a new beginning and things would change for the better. Hope Marie York put on the deep red Prada suit that cost her nearly two months pay from her job back in Florence, Oregon. After two years of planning and saving, the day had finally come for her to start over. Her closet was filled with designer clothing, in her small New York City studio apartment, and her expensive salon makeover had left her almost unrecognizable from the plain small town girl she left behind in Oregon. With a deep breath, she opened the door and walked to meet Shauna at the small café that had become their unofficial meeting spot.

"My lord Hope, look at you!" Shauna said with a slow gaze up and down that I may have resented if I hadn't been so thrilled to see Shauna's mouth hanging open. I'd always admired Shauna's style and confidence, perhaps even being a tiny bit jealous of how much of those qualities oozed out of her without effort. Knowing from her expression that I had impressed her gave me a jolt of confidence I needed on my first day. Shauna, although my best friend since 4th grade, could be a bit of a bitch and I knew it took a lot to make her jaw drop these days. Tall, fit, blonde hair and blue eyes with legs a mile long. Shauna could piss off Barbie, because Ken's head would surely turn to follow her as she walked by.

"Thanks Shauna, just seeing your expression almost makes the agony of the last two years of planning and saving worth it!"

Two years ago, I would have gone unnoticed. I was average. Not too tall, not too short. Mousey dirty blonde hair, pale complexion and an extra ten pounds put me at around a five on the rating scale. My green eyes hidden behind glasses that concealed my lack of makeup. It didn't help that my wardrobe consisted of only black, white, brown and navy. My closets were lined with conservative sweater sets, dark colored slacks, jeans, plain t-shirts and sensible flats. But today, Shauna's face told me that I looked the part of at least an eight. In two years, I had worked hard to transform myself. A strict diet and exercise routine helped shed 15 pounds and defined my muscles. Bright blonde highlights and a magician haircutter transformed my thick hair into bright layers. A good lesson in using makeup to accentuate my almond shaped green eyes and full lips, along with trading my glasses for contacts, completed my physical makeover. Two years of saving transformed my wardrobe from drab to designer and even I thought I looked the part of a New York City professional woman.

"We need to head to the bar and celebrate after your big first day today." Shauna could truly find a reason to head to the bar and celebrate for anything. But today I wasn't going to argue because I was counting on feeling as good at the end of the first day of my new job as I did at the beginning of it.

"How about if we meet at that ritzy bar they have in your hotel after work? The one on the 45th floor that overlooks the city, Icon, I think it's called. I'm sure the drinks are expensive, but we can find some horny traveling salesman to buy them for us!"

I almost choked on my yogurt at her description of who tonight's wallet would belong to for us. But Shauna was right; there was never a shortage of men waiting to buy our drinks with the way Shauna looked.

"I don't know if it's such a good idea for us to party in the hotel I am working at on my very first day. I wouldn't want to people to see me and think I was a party girl." I offered an alternative. "How about we go to Marley's Pub instead?"

Shauna gave a small wave to the handsome man clearly drooling at her from the table across from us and said loud enough for most of the café to hear "No, we are going to Icon tonight and I won't take no for an answer. The old Hope goes to Marley's Pub, the new Hope goes to Icon to be seen." Finishing her breakfast and standing, clearly not a topic she was planning on discussing, Shauna took three steps and looked back "Icon 6:00 tonight". Then she winked at the drooling man listening to our conversation intently and I wondered if she was hoping me or the stranger would be at Icon tonight when she arrived.

Chapter 2

Blowing an escaped strand of hair off my face, I stopped outside to look at the magnificent hotel where I would now spend my days. The Monet, one of only two five star hotels in a city where a two star hotel can cost more than three hundred dollars a night, is one of the most grand buildings in all of the city. Stone columns arching more than three stories high set the tone for the entry of the 45 story grand structure. The doorman smiled at me as I took it all in, opening the door tipping his hat to me, "Good morning and Welcome to The Monet". Although I had been inside the building for two interviews, the lobby still struck me with awe as I entered the Upper East Side iconic hotel.

Like stepping back in time, the lobby of the Monet brought together old world luxury with modern sleekness. Immaculate marble and gleaming crystal were offset by breathtaking vibrant colored flower arrangements on an unimaginable scale. Oversized archways and vaulted ceilings held grand crystal chandeliers that sparkled. A sweeping staircase, the epitome of elegance, set the backdrop for the understated reception desk.

I was almost an hour early for the beginning of my first day, even after breakfast with Shauna. I tried not to walk around the lobby too starry eyed, but it was hard to contain my excitement of landing my dream job. With all of my new outward changed, I had hoped to blend in with all the other young professional native New Yorkers working at the magnificent hotel. But even without all my outward changes, inside I still felt like the plain girl from Oregon.

I had to really work at pretending I belonged there as I walked to the general manager's office to report for my first day as The Monet's new event coordinator. Four years of college studying hospitality and business, three years as an assistant event coordinator in the largest hotel in Oregon, a brand new wardrobe, makeover, city and apartment and I still felt unworthy of the job. Why couldn't I have Shauna's sense of belonging? It took her all of about 30 minutes to feel at home in New York when she moved almost four years ago at the age of twenty two.

It wasn't just Shauna that had the innate sense of belonging wherever she went. My uber gorgeous step mother Candace, the former Miss Oregon, had the same sense of belonging that I clearly missed out on. My dad, Joe York, a retired secret service officer, had a different kind of confidence than his wife, his wasn't showy. His was a quiet confidence, the kind that made you stand straighter when he was in the room. Of course, my beyond beautiful two step sisters also reaped the benefits from belonging to two confident parents and took confidence to a whole new level that some people would no longer call confident but instead call entitlement.

***

George Windham, the general manager, was a forty something, roundish balding man that I looked forward to working for. He seemed kind and well mannered and I believed him when he told me that he would help me become a success in my new position. After a grand tour of the hotel and introductions to at least fifty employees, he left me with the reception manager for my first day of hotel training. Even though I was going to be the hotel's event planner, the hotel had a policy of all new employees spending their first month training in the key positions of the hotel so that they truly understood how the hotel worked. My first week would be spent in reception, learning the check in and check out process.

George left me with Dylan, the outgoing red headed reception manager, who gave me an overview and then we took a break together to grab some coffee. "So, are you single Hope? Because this hotel is better than any singles bar for hunting wealthy bachelors. I mean, when a man can spend seven hundred dollars a night on a hotel, he can afford to keep me stocked in my Jimmy Choos, right?"

Dylan laughed as she studied me from across the table. Despite my surprise at hearing that a manager thinks of her position as a hunting ground, I couldn't help but think that Dylan would have no problem finding a handsome bachelor of her own. Unlike me, Dylan was sex on a stick with an abundance of curves and sparkle. Although tiny, I'd bet men didn't notice her height. She wore a plunging purple halter top barely containing her D cups under her snug fitting reception blazer. Her face looked like it was airbrushed with perfect makeup to suit her large brown eyes. Although to my liking it was a bit Dolly Parton over the top, I could definitely see the appeal that she would have over men.

The rest of the morning flew by with me observing the reception staff as they did their work. By late afternoon Dylan announced that it was time for me to graduate and take a turn at checking in the next guest. I'd just hung up the phone after transferring a guest to the concierge to make some reservations, when I looked up to see the next guest approaching the desk for check in. My heart skipped a beat and I stuttered "Wwwww..Welcome to The Monet, how may I help you?" I looked up to the most amazing pale blue eyes surrounded by dark black eyelashes that I have ever seen. Instantly I felt my face flush and silently cursed my pale skin.

"You must be new here" the Adonis standing before me said in a deep, smooth voice.

"Ummm.... I apologize, I am new but I will do my best to get you checked in quickly." Flushing even more as I realized that he was able to see my inexperience.

"I wasn't worried about a speedy check in, I meant I would have remembered you if I had seen you here before."

My lips and mouth went dry and I had trouble speaking. Wait, did he just flirt with me? Blinking out of my daze, I licked my dry lips and looked up at the beautiful man, who was staring at my mouth, seemingly unfazed by my bumbling motions.

This was not a beautiful man; this was a walking work of art. Tall, dark and handsome couldn't begin to describe what stood before me. His bone structure looked as if it was created from the chisel and stone of an artist. His straight strong nose, stood above perfect full lips and his slight smile revealed two glorious cavernous dimples that sent a tingle straight through my spine just seeing a hint of them. His light blue dress shirt neatly pressed with a beautiful blue and gray tie, and low hanging dark gray dress pants, all looked as if they were custom made for him.

" Kennedy Jenner, Mrs….." the beautiful man said as he extended his hand in my direction.

"It's *Miss* Hope York, Mr. Jenner, nice to meet you." A shock of electricity shot through my body as his large hand enveloped mine. My heartbeat raced and all of the hair on my body rose, despite my best effort to hide my excitement.

He held my hand for longer than necessary for a standard handshake and stared into my eyes with one brow arched and the hint of a dimple desperate to escape. "Are you feeling okay Miss York?"

Mortified, I was aware that my face had to match the deep red color of my suit by now, but I sputtered out a response. "I'm fine Mr. Jenner."

I was upset with myself for not being able to hide my nerves and for allowing a man I didn't know turn me to jello. Yet, he stood there with his cocky expression not wavering in his focus to allow me a few seconds to compose myself. I stumbled with the computer keys and pulled up the amazing creatures' reservation. "I'll just need a credit card and a license to check you in Mr. Jenner." I continued to look down at the computer screen as he grabbed for his wallet, but I could feel his gaze slowly taking in my face and its reactions to him. Finally, after what seemed like ten minutes of keypunching, but was in reality probably only thirty seconds, I completed the check in and offered Mr. Jenner the room card.

He took the room cards from my hand, his thumb brushing against mine in the exchange and there it was again, the unmistakable electricity traveling to places that no man has gone in quite some time. Too long, I suddenly realized. "Enjoy your stay Mr. Jenner." I managed a smile.

"Oh, I will enjoy my stay this time, Ms. York, you can count on it."

I nodded, although I had no idea what that was supposed to mean. I watched as the most beautiful man I had ever laid eyes on walked toward the elevator. I saw him smile without looking my way as he stepped into the car and my knees went weak.

I felt the flood of relief from the release of the intensity Kennedy Jenner had brought upon. Yet, I also felt oddly sad that he was now gone. Dylan, obviously not one to miss much that happens when a handsome man approaches her reception desk, whistled a sexy catcall from behind me.

"Jesus, Hope, you couldn't cut the sexual tension in that exchange with a hatchet!"

Had I really just made an ass out of myself on my first day at my dream job in front of a man way out of my league? I smiled politely to Dylan and excused myself to go the ladies room to compose myself back to the professional I was supposed to be.

The remainder of the day was uneventful, although I did find myself staring at the elevator bank on one too many occasions. Thank the Lord that man came in late in the day, or I would have been unable to function for the entire day.

Chapter 3

Shauna was already seated at the bar when I walked into Icon. The bar was truly a spectacular sight. On one side, floor to ceiling windows displayed the entire city from the bar's perch upon the 45th floor of The Monet. The other side was a wall of glass leading to an outside deck boasting mahogany outdoor lounge chairs that were set up in intimate arrangements to allow for small groups to talk. The deck displayed two outdoor bars and I could hear jazz playing and voices laughing in the distance.

"Hope!" Shauna's loud bubbly display of excitement caused some of the men that were watching Shauna to look my way. I walked to the bar, again slightly flushed, and hugged Shauna, happy to see a familiar face after a long first day. "Well, how was it? Find any hot men to seduce at work?"

We talked and laughed about my day and at some point, I made the mistake of telling her about the Adonis I had met. If I was what could be considered a prude, Shauna would be the exact opposite. Always ready to openly discuss sexual encounters and her love of men in general. Me, on the other hand, generally didn't have much to discuss.

After a few drinks and Shauna's playfully teasing me to print an extra key and slip into the handsome guest's room for a little excitement, I convinced her it was time to go. Linking arms, we headed toward the door, where I promptly walked directly into him.

He grinned, showing a hint of the dimples that made my knees go weak and stared down at me "I told you I was going to have a good stay this time." I froze, unable to respond, and just stared at him like a love struck teenager. Why did I respond like such an idiot around this man? Kennedy put his arm out to place his hand on my shoulder and reached down so that I could feel his breath on my ear, "Please, have a drink with me Miss York."

Shauna giggled and quickly interjected "I really have to go, but you should stay for a little while and enjoy that drink Hope". Kennedy smiled at Shauna, but I noticed that he didn't look her up and down as all men do when meeting her.

"Ummm....I really have to get going, I have an appointment I need to get to."

Kennedy smiled down at me and released my shoulder. Leaning closer until I could feel the heat resonating from his body and I felt my own body start to tingle, he whispered "I only take no for an answer once, so I will see you again soon Ms. York."

"What in the world happened in there?" Shauna screeched as we entered the elevator for the ride down to the street. "From the look on your face, I take it that was the guy from this afternoon?" She pushed the buttons staring at me, apparently it wasn't a rhetorical question and she was awaiting a response.

"Yes, that was the man from reception today. I have no idea what comes over me when I am near that man. It's like my brain turns to mush and I can't control my body!"

Shauna looked irritated "Hope, one look at the way that man looks at you and I can tell you that you do not need to control your body. That man is going to do it for you! Why on earth didn't you accept his invitation to have a drink?"

As the doors opened to the lobby level, I couldn't help but wonder why I didn't accept his invitation either. As we walked through the lobby a few of the employees waived goodnight and I was glad for the relief from Shauna's inquisition for a moment.

Out on the street, the fresh air and bustling sounds of the city brought me back to reality. "I have no idea Shauna, I think I may be afraid of the man a little. Not in the violent-afraid sort of way, but in the 'he makes me melt like butter on a roof in Arizona type of way!'"

After another short lecture on the benefits of casual sex, and reminding me that I moved to New York to start a new, better life, Shauna hugged me and we agreed to meet at Icon again Thursday after work.

***

The next two days passed in a blur as I worked to learn everything I could about the hotel and all of the different jobs that keep the hotel rated with five stars. Although I kept myself busy, my eyes were always on the lookout for the Adonis. Unfortunately, I didn't see him, and because I checked him in, I knew that he was checking out soon.

Chapter 4

Kennedy Jenner never obsessed over anything other than business. He made a fortune by keeping a clear head and controlling his emotions. He believed that timing was everything and he often won deals because he paid attention to details and knew when to strike a deal and when to back off. As the founder of Jenner Holdings, he had more than three thousand employees that relied on him and he took the responsibility very seriously. His diverse business investments and financial security provided him with a lifestyle that most would envy. Women threw themselves at him either because of his looks or his money, sometimes both. If they wanted to give him their body so easily, who was he to refuse?

Yet today as he ran on the treadmill at The Monet, he couldn't think of anything other than little Miss Hope York. Running usually soothed him and cleared his head, but today the more his heart raced and sweat poured off his body, all he could think of was getting sweaty with the little clerk. As he ratcheted up the speed, he shook his head thinking of her flawless skin and big pouty lips. The harder he ran the more he realized he needed to go find that little woman and get himself into her bed so he can get her out of his head.

Kennedy showered and changed and went upstairs to Icon, hoping that maybe she would be there again. He had gone up to Icon every night after their first meeting, but she was never anywhere to be found.

***

Shauna and Hope sat out on the deck at Icon enjoying the warm fall evening. Two very handsome men bought them drinks and settled in next to them attempting to charm them with wit and good smiles.

Kennedy stood at the bar ordering a drink and scanned the room for Hope. Disappointed, he headed outside onto the deck to get some air and clear his head. As he reached for the door leading to the outside deck, he saw her. Head thrown back laughing, she was even more beautiful than he remembered. Her deep green blouse and skirt made her instantly stand out amongst the crowd. But who was the bozo sitting too close to her making her laugh? Realizing he had the door lever in a death grip, he composed himself before walking over to Hope.

"Miss York, I'm having a problem with the hotel and was wondering if you could provide some assistance?" Startled by the voice that could only belong to him, Hope turned and looked up into the pale blue eyes that made her knees weak. They studied each other for a moment and then she saw the slight uptick in his mouth and a hint of a dimple craving to make an appearance.

"Umm, yes Mr. Jenner, let me see if I can provide assistance."

As she stood to walk away from Shauna and the two men, one stood with her and smiled. "I'll be here waiting for you when you are done Hope".

Barely able to contain himself, Kennedy took two steps to face the smiling man and stood toe to toe, towering over the man until the poor man's smile disappeared. "She won't be coming back."

Shauna smiled and giggled and gave her friend a wink and a quick hug.

***

Kennedy put his hand on the small of my back and led me out of the bar. The heat from his light touch radiated through my body and his fingers scorched the skin where they touched. Out in the hall, I again flushed with an odd mix of embarrassment and desire, and was unable to look into his eyes. "What seems to be the problem, Mr. Jenner?" I whispered, unable to find my full voice.

"The problem is that I haven't had any dessert yet and I was wondering if you would join me." His beautiful face was serious, the only glimpse of honesty was an ever so slight upward turn on the left side of his smile that caused the irrepressible dimple to start to show.

"Are you saying that you took me away from my best friend and our two new friends under false pretenses?"

Kennedy didn't speak for a moment, then asked "Are you sleeping with anyone?" The way he asked the question was so direct but relaxed, he could have been asking for directions.

The question caught me so off guard, I stared up at him in confusion. "Am I sleeping with someone?"

He took one step closer, "Yes, that is the question I asked. Would you like to know if I am sleeping with anyone before you answer?"

I took one step back and a deep breath. "Why is it any of your business if I am sleeping with anyone Mr. Jenner?"

Another step closer and his beautiful face bent to my ear "Because I want to be the only one fucking you, Hope." My knees weakened and I pulled my head up so fast to look up at him that I began to sway, unsteady in my balance. He took one step closer and I took another back until I hit the wall behind me. Placing one hand on each side of my head, he smiled, the full dimple smile this time and I felt an ache between my thighs.

Knowing the old Hope would have been terrified and ran away made my response easier. "No, I am not currently sleeping with anyone." We stared into each other's eyes for a long minute and for a second I thought he would kiss me. Instead, he lifted my hand to his mouth, flattened my hand and kissed my palm until I felt just a hint of tongue in the center of my palm. Did he just taste me? Before I could think, he took my hand and led me into the elevator. I realized I was not breathing and forced an exhale as we stood in the elevator waiting for the doors to close. Him behind me close enough to feel his breathing. I was half expecting him to push the button for the 44th floor, as I knew what floor his room was on.   I was slightly disappointed, yet relieved, when he pushed the button to go down to the lobby.

Standing so close to me, I took a deep breath in and smelled him.   Soap and musk – it made me want to taste him right back. As I stepped forward when the elevator doors opened, the closeness of his body was replaced by his hand again at the small of my back. Without speaking, he guided us through the lobby and out to the street.

"Where are we going?" I glanced a look at him for the first time since we left the 45th floor.

"To see if this can work" he responded in his deep velvety voice and took my hand in his. I suppose I should have been nervous or concerned for my safety. But I wasn't. I just hoped that wherever it was we were going was a small space like the elevator where we would need to stand close again.

We walked for a few blocks before reaching a small, old fashioned ice cream shop. He opened the door and motioned for me to walk in. "A booth for two, preferably private."

The hostess with tremendous breasts peeking out from her costume designed to look like a girl from the fifties stared at the Adonis, her mouth hanging open for a few seconds before regaining her composure. I seemed to have been the only one to notice the striking hostess offering her ample breasts and attention to Kennedy, his gaze never left me. We followed her to a booth in the back of the small parlor and I sat across from him, missing his touch as soon as he released my hand.

He stared across the table holding my eyes, not allowing me to look away. "I am attracted to you Hope. I can give you anything you want, I want one thing in return." My eyes closed knowing what would come next. They all want only one thing. I forced myself to open my eyes and the close proximity of him and his intense focus heightened to a physically painful level. I shifted re-crossing my legs in a fruitless attempt to contain the throb settling in between my thighs. A hint of an upward tilt bared the start of that left dimple telling me he knew what I was feeling.

"And what if I don't want to give you the one thing you want, Mr. Jenner?"

He stared, his pale blue eyes darkening to steel with intensity. "Kiss me before you decide what you are willing to give me."

My breath turning to pants at his words, I licked my lips and watched his gaze settle in on my mouth. My body was betraying my mind. He groaned lifting his gaze back to my eyes, reached over the small table and put his hand firmly behind my neck, pulling me closer to him over the table. Before my brain could catch up with my body, his lips covered mine. Hard confident pressure with just enough aggressive force to demand my lips open when his tongue licked my lips. He growled, tilting his head to deepen the kiss, his tongue dipped inside my mouth, tasting me in long sensual strokes. I felt my clit swell and my heart pound against my chest. His release softened and he ended the kiss with a nip to my bottom lip that was stronger than a friendly bite but not quite painful. Our faces still close, nose against nose, ragged breathing, "I want no lies, Hope, ever."

That is the one thing that he wants? Certainly not what I expected. I was vaguely aware of the waitress standing with her jaw again hanging open as she cleared her throat to bring us back to reality. Embarrassed by the intrusion into our private moment, I pulled back and attempted to settle myself back into my seat. He ordered something that earned him a big smile from the large breasted waitress, but my brain was not capable of stringing the words he spoke together. I needed to clear my head and move the focus back to the typical "getting to know you" date type conversation before I did something stupid.

"So, Mr. Jenner, what brings you to New York?" The now familiar flush quickly creeping up over my face. What is it about this man that makes me turn red every time I am near him?

"Business. And although I like the thought of you calling me Mr. Jenner when you are underneath me in the bedroom, I think Kennedy is more appropriate at the moment, don't you?"

Surely he didn't just say that, did he? "Excuse me?" Eyebrows furrowing in confusion at his question.

He leaned in closer and slowly, with slight hint of amusement "You heard me correctly Hope, Kennedy now, Mr. Jenner in the future."

"Umm..., do you come to the City often?"

A slow confident smile spread across his face and my breath caught at the vision of the beautiful full smile, dimples so deep I had to remember to breathe. "I do now, Hope." Again interrupted by the full breasted waitress, this time it was a relief. The smile so soon after our kiss and my traitorous body's reaction to him left me in a state that was difficult to keep up with our conversation.

The waitress turned and handed me a large chocolate ice cream cone covered in red sprinkles, then she was gone. "Where is your dessert?" His eyebrows arched and slight smile turned carnal "My dessert is watching you eat that."

At first, I had a horrible vision in my head of how stupid I must look slowly licking the ice cream cone. But his unwavering gaze and beautiful pale eyes turned almost navy with desire gave me the confidence I needed to push back the old Hope and become the new woman I so desperately needed to be. I closed my eyes and took a few long slow strokes with the flat of my tongue bringing the ice cream into my mouth and suckling it before a deep swallow.

"Jesus Christ." His eyes bore into me, both hands fisting through his hair harshly. "I want to fuck you so bad it hurts." I was aroused at the thought of having such control over such an incredibly beautiful man.

When I finished the dessert, he abruptly stood, throwing some cash on the table. The reality of my teasing behavior flooded back to me and I was thoroughly embarrassed. Never in my life did I act that way before, especially in such a public place. Kennedy grabbed my hand and walked with long strides toward the door. I was barely able to keep up. Outside, his longing gaze was replaced with a stone, unreadable face. "I'd like to make sure you get home safely, if that's okay." It was still early and a few minutes earlier I thought the last thing he wanted to do was end the evening, but something had changed.

Embarrassed, but forcing myself to hold my head high. "I can walk from here. Thank you for dessert Kennedy."

"You will not walk alone." His tone clearly leaving no room for disagreement, I pointed north and explained that I was five blocks up and two streets over. He took a deep breath and gently took my hand and began walking. He was so close to me, yet the distance that came between us made it feel like we were miles apart. We arrived at my building, a four story brownstone, and made our way up the ten stairs to the doorway. I explained that my studio was on the ground floor and he made no attempt to join me inside.

"Is that your bedroom window right there? You have no security on it."

I didn't want to admit that I was uncomfortable with the lack of security and had planned on adding an alarm, but couldn't since I had spent all of my savings on my new wardrobe. "The window has a lock on it."

He stared down at me with a look I couldn't quite identify. Was it concern or anger? I reached for the door knob and began to say thank you once again. Stepping in front of me to block my entrance, he put both hands on my shoulders and pulled me close. His mouth covering mine, his lips and kiss were gentle this time. A soft caress that sparked tenderness, different from the passionate, wanting kiss from earlier. He released my lips and put his forehead to mine, touching his finger to my mouth. "Good night Hope".

I gave a slight smile and waited until he backed off slightly. Turning to walk into the building, I looked back over my shoulder and had no idea where the word came from. "Yes."

Walking down the steps, he halted and turned to look back at me, eyebrows furrowed in confusion. "Yes?"

"Yes, to your one request."

He smiled, the full blown make your knees weak smile with dimples the size of the Grand Canyon. I smiled back and turned into my building without looking back, knowing his eyes were on my ass, until I was out of his view.

Chapter 5

"Okay, spill it girly." Although we didn't speak or make plans for breakfast on Friday morning, I knew Shauna would be at our café after my unexpected departure from Icon last night. After all these years, we were like an old married couple who knew what the other was thinking before she said it.

"I have no idea what happened, one minute we were caught in intense sexual tension, the next he was walking me home and I was taking a cold shower."

"Forget the shower part; I want to hear about the sexual tension part." Shauna was a professional basketball team cheerleader, but she should have been a detective. She had a way of getting all the information out of you while making you feel somehow guilty if you keep anything back.

"There really isn't much to tell. We went for ice cream and he kissed me until I wasn't sure of my own name for few minutes. Then he walked me home without saying a word and gave me a gentle kiss without even asking to come in."

"Are you going to see him again?"

"I don't think so, he lives in Chicago and he is checking out today. It's probably a good thing nothing happened last night."

Shauna was silent, nodded and looked at her watch, signaling she needed to leave. "Tonight, 6pm. Forget Icon, let's try out that new club Salt that opened on 57th. I'll meet you in the lobby of the hotel."

I really didn't want to go. My head was cluttered and I had the desire to put on sweatpants and settle in with a bucket of Ben and Jerry's and a sappy movie. But no, that's old Hope. "Okay, I'm game." I gave her my best fake smile and took off to the hotel.

***

Today would be my last day of training at the reception desk. The morning was busy with guest check outs, but I looked up every time I hear the elevator ding and was disappointed each time. Dylan must have realized what I was doing. "If you're looking for that gorgeous man that got your attention on Monday, he checked out before you arrived. He mentioned something about an early morning flight. I know you saw him first, but I wouldn't mind helping him fluff his pillows in his suite...that man is beyond sexy."

I tried to hide my disappointment. "Oh, I wasn't looking for a guest, I wanted to speak to George about where I would be training next week and thought he might come by."

Completely deflated with no contact before he left, I still couldn't help but think about him all day. By late afternoon, I was glad that Shauna had insisted we got out tonight. A few drinks and some dancing is probably what I needed to get Kennedy Jenner out of my mind.

Almost at the end of my day, an older man in a suit approached the counter holding an envelope. "I'm looking for Ms. York".

I accepted the envelope and he waited. Was he waiting for a tip? Reaching for my pocketbook, I fished out a few dollars and extended my hand in his direction. The older gentleman smiled and shook his head. "No, Ms. York, I believe you should read the card."

Inside, on thick cream stationery with gold leaf lettering I saw the initials KJ. My spine straightened and heartbeat quickened at just knowing he wrote the note. *Dear Hope, Charles is my driver when I am in New York. Please allow him to drive you home this evening. He has a gift in his car that needs to be delivered to your apartment with you. Kennedy.* A business card was also included in the envelope, where he had handwritten in his cell phone number.

Shauna arrived and made her way to the reception desk a few steps away from Charles. "There has been a small change in plans Shauna. This is Charles." I motioned toward the smiling older gentlemen dressed in a chauffer's suit and cap. "Kennedy has sent him to drive me to my apartment along with a gift that he has in the car for me. "

"Oh, I'm so excited! I knew that man couldn't just walk away from you!" Shauna turned her charm to Charles. "Charles, would you mind terribly bringing Hope to meet me after she delivers the gift to her apartment?"

Charles may have been older but Shauna's charm was not lost on the man. "No problem ma'am."

"Hope, I would go with you, especially because I am dying to find out what the gift is, but I told a few of the girls from the squad that we would meet them at Salt in fifteen minutes and, since I know the bouncer, I promised I'd get us all in for free." After a quick air kiss she walked toward the lobby exit with every man's eyes following the sway of her hips, including old Charles.

As I climbed into the back of the stretch limousine and provided Charles with my address, I saw a large package wrapped in brown paper with another handwritten card attached. Perhaps I could find out more about Kennedy from Charles if he has been his driver for years? "Charles, how long have you known Mr. Jenner?"

"Probably about five years in total, he uses my services exclusively when he is in New York." Charles sounded proud in his statement.

"How often does he come to New York?"

"Usually once a month, sometimes for a day trip, other times he spends a few days."

Feeling my heartbeat speed up at the possibility of seeing Kennedy again, I felt like I was back in high school. I sagged back into my seat and curiously considered what was under the brown paper. It was shaped like a picture of some sort, although it was pretty large for a picture. As we pulled up to my brownstone, I realized it would be difficult for me to maneuver the large package into the house by myself. Charles opened the door and put his hand out to help me out of the car.

"Mr. Jenner gave me specific instructions that I am to carry the gift into your apartment for you."

Walking up the stairs to my brownstone, I noticed something was different, but couldn't quite put my finger on it. As I got closer to the front door, I realized that my window was now partially covered in beautiful antique decorative wrought iron. The design was elegant and graceful almost concealing the true purpose of its placement as a decorative work of art. Security. It would be impossible for anyone to fit through my window with the iron bars carefully placed to limit accessibility. I had seen window coverings like these when I was researching security, but antique pieces like that were thousands of dollars and a luxury I could never afford. My first thought was that the landlord had added the security, but then I remembered Kennedy's statement about my lack of security the night before.

I opened the door to my apartment and Charles carefully placed the package on the table and returned to his car telling me to take as much time as I needed. Two seconds after I closed the door behind him, I tore through the brown paper like a child on Christmas morning, curiosity finally getting the better of my composure. Underneath, the most striking work of art I have ever seen took my breath away. Not quite abstract, but bright colors and dimension shaded a simple picture of woman's tongue eating an ice cream cone. There was no face attached to the tongue and it was almost difficult to make out the tongue licking the cone behind the bold splashes of color and strokes of dimensions. Sexual. Sensual. Raw. The feelings that looking at the work of art evoked were powerful. Tears stung my eyes and I forced my lids to shut to keep them at bay.

Then I remembered there was another card on the outside. I searched through the wrapping and found it. *Hang this original so that you can see it from your bed. I've purchased the print to hang in my bedroom. KJ.*

Oh. My. Lord. Who is this man? I really didn't know him, but yet it felt like I had been waiting forever for him to arrive. My heart raced and my smile spread so wide that it hurt. I had to call and say thank you, I couldn't wait to hear his voice. I dialed the cell phone number that he wrote on his business card.

"Kennedy." The response from the other end of the phone on the first ring.

"Oh, hello Kennedy, this is Hope York." God, why am I such a dork? I had to recite my first and last name to identify myself to a man that I kissed last night and sent me an amazing gift today. I inwardly cringed at my uncoolness.

"Hope, did you get home safely?" I could hear the smile in his voice.

"Yes, I did. It was very sweet of you to send Charles and the artwork is, well...it's just amazing. I mean it's beautiful."

"I'm glad you like it. I thought it was beautiful too. Although it doesn't come close to watching the real thing in person last night." I was about to say, *Thank you,* when his deep voice interrupted my thought. "Charles tells me that your friend asked him to drop you off at a club to meet her this evening."

"Ummm....yes, I didn't mean to ask for a ride, it just sort of happened."

The velvet sound of Kennedy's deep voice and a deep laugh gave me relief that he was not annoyed that I was taking advantage of his generosity. "Hope, I don't want you to go the club tonight. I want you to stay home and masturbate and think about me."

Jesus. Even through the phone this man could make my nipples harden with excitement. I let him wait in silence for a minute. If anyone else had spoken those same words to me I would be outraged. Yet Kennedy's words spoken as a command, and not a request, created a desire to obey him that filled me. "Okay." The word came out of my own mouth and yet I was shocked that I had just agreed to do what he commanded.

"Good, thank you."

"And what will *you* be doing tonight while I am home in my bed alone?" I smiled, not quite sure what I wanted his response to be.

"Not what I usually do on a Friday night." Silence for a moment, and then "I'll call you tomorrow, I need to make a few calls to change some previous commitments. "

A few minutes later, I hung up the phone. At the window, I saw Charles on his cell phone and then he smiled and pulled away. I felt as though we had just agreed to a lot of things in our short conversation, yet I wasn't quite positive what those things were. My cell phone buzzed and I realized that I needed to let Shauna know that I wasn't going to meet her at the club. It was easier to feign a sudden illness then to tell Shauna the truth. That I had committed to a man that I barely knew that I would stay in my apartment and masturbate just didn't come through well in a text.

Chapter 6

Kennedy Jenner had a standing date with Mikayla Santorina every Friday night for the last three months. It wasn't a complicated relationship. Mikayla liked to go out to expensive dinners and socialize at parties and be seen on the arm of a tall dark, handsome and wealthy man. Kennedy frequently needed a date to social events that he was required to attend in his business. And, at the end of the night, he liked to get fucked or sucked and then go home alone without the pressure of sleepovers and mornings after with a woman. Mikayla had tried on more than one occasion to make the arrangement into something more, but Kennedy made it clear he was not interested in more.

Tonight he cancelled their plans to attend the Mayor's charity dinner together, by telling Mikayla that he had a business emergency that he needed to attend to. It was easier than telling her the truth, and if things didn't work out with little Miss York, he might see fit to maintain their arrangement.

Mikayla was not happy when Kennedy called to cancel, but offered to meet him after the dinner for the customary second half of their date night anyway. Not even tempted, he declined her offer.

***

Being wealthy and handsome had made him a target for women. He only dated the ones that knew the rules and could provide only what he needed and be happy with what little he could offer. Kennedy's time and energy were devoted to building his company over the past eight years. There was no time left for distractions. He wouldn't allow it. Either he controlled the relationship or he ended the relationship. The same rules applied in his business. Control was not something he could give up, he needed it to survive.

Kennedy's assistant Marcy was not surprised that he called so late in the day. But she was surprised that he called to make arrangements for two additional deliveries to a woman in New York. And the fact that he called at a time when he was supposed to be out with Mikayla put a smile on Marcy's face. Marcy didn't trust Mikayla and hoped that the relationship would soon end.

Chapter 7

The buzzer sounded as I was getting dressed to go to the gym and I peeked out the window to see who could be at the door so early on a Saturday morning. Charles stood in full uniform and removed his cap with a smile, greeting me with a slight bow. In his left arm was a large flower box. "Good morning Ms. York".

I opened the door. "Good Morning Charles, this is an unexpected visit."

Charles extended his arms to pass me the box he was carrying. "Mr. Jenner asked that I deliver these to you and see that you are driven on any errands you need to run today."

I smiled and offered him to come in, but he politely declined. "I was just getting ready to go to the gym, if you don't mind waiting; I'll be ready in a few minutes."

"Take all the time you need Miss York, I'm yours for the day."

***

Charles dropped me off back at my apartment after a morning at the gym, followed by running half a dozen errands that would have taken me twice as long on the subway. Opening the door to my apartment, the smell of two dozen lilac and yellow roses filled the air. I closed my eyes and smiled, opening to gaze at the beautiful, erotic picture now hanging just four feet from the foot of my bed.

Later that evening Kennedy called and we spoke longer this time. I told him about my new job, my move from Oregon, and a little about Shauna. The conversation seemed oddly normal and familiar. I didn't ask him what he did the night before and he didn't ask me.

The next week flew by and, although I spoke to Kennedy every day, I didn't ask when he was coming back to the city. I wanted to know but was afraid to ask, although I was not quite sure why.

***

Friday afternoon as I was getting ready to leave work, my cell phone rang and I smiled seeing his number. "Hi."

"Are you on birth control?" His voice was deep and tone even. I could tell it was asked a serious question and not a flirty game. He wanted a serious answer. Flush seeped up my face. The man could make me blush with only a word on the phone.

Through the corner of my eye, I saw the hotel manager, George, heading my way. "Umm...yes I am, but could we possibly talk about this later, I'd rather not have my boss know about my sex life, or lack thereof, and he is walking right toward me."

"We can continue this conversation later, but I am happy to know about your 'lack thereof' of a sex life." I could hear him smiling smugly through the phone. I bet that response earned a visit from both dimples.

George arrived and we hung up. "Hope, I'm sorry to ask so late on a Friday, but there is a VIP in the Penthouse suite that wants to discuss holding a large event here."

"No problem George, I'm happy to do it."

I sent a quick text to Shauna to tell her about the change in plans and to go on to happy hour without me.

***

I'd toured the penthouse suite on my first day when it was vacant and knew that it was luxe. It occupied almost half of an entire floor and there was a parlor and dining room where we could sit and discuss planning an event. I buzzed the suite and looked over the folder George had given me containing some basics on the event. No name in the file. I'd have to introduce myself and hope the guest offered their name in return.

The door opened and my jaw dropped. Kennedy. I was stunned and couldn't move. Amusement danced in his eyes as he stared down at me, giving me the smile AND dimples. My knees went weak and I stood there like a school girl, nervous and unable to smile back. Two quick strides and he was in my personal space. "I couldn't wait any longer to see you."

He lifted my hand and pulled it to his mouth. His amused eyes gone and replaced by intense focus. His eyes didn't leave mine as he brought us two steps forward into the room and I vaguely heard the door close behind me. He leaned down, tucking his head into my hair and gently kissed my neck. The feel of his lips on the tender skin brought goose bumps all over my body. My nipples perked and arousal shot through me.

"Hi." Was the best I could force out of my lungs.

"Hi beautiful." He gently pinned me against the wall behind me, capturing my mouth. Softness quickly turning to passion. I loved the way he kissed me as if he had to in order to breathe. He stole the air from my lungs. He nibbled on my bottom lip slowly going from one corner to the other. I sucked his tongue. He responded by pressing his body firmly into mine. I could feel his erection hard against my belly. I wrapped my arms around his broad shoulders and lifted one leg around his hip to feel more of him. A low moan escaping as he pressed his body harder into me.

Kennedy pulled back, and looked down at my face. I could see his chest rise and fall quickly as he fought to regain some control. "Fuck Hope, I need to have you."

I looked into his eyes for a few seconds and made a decision. I nodded, unable to find words. He watched me intently as I ran my hands along his chest feeling the hard muscle I had only envisioned were there. I tugged at the bottom and released the hem of his tucked dress shirt. His eyes never leaving my face, I could see him searching my eyes to confirm the answer I had already given him.

He lifted me up and carried me to the bedroom, sitting me on the edge of the bed. He took two steps back and looked down at me. "Undress for me." I slowly unbuttoned my deep blue silk shirt, allowing it to fall open revealing my deep blue lace bra. "Jesus, Hope" he whispered in a husky low voice, but made no movement toward me.

I stood, slowly unzipping my skirt and let it drop to the floor around me. Matching lace blue boy short panties revealed. I sat and slowly unbuckled the straps from my high heeled sandals, and then I stood. His eyes drank me in slowly from head to toe. When his eyes reached mine, a slight smile and an arch of one eyebrow. "Your turn."

I wasn't going to get the slow teasing strip tease I had just given him. He closed the space between us and smiled down at me. A wicked smile that made my knees weak. I was never so turned on in my entire life.

"I'm going to watch as I make you cum and then pump my cum so far into you that you can feel it seep through your body for days."

My clit swelled at his words and their intensity brought me to the cliff of orgasm. "I'm going to taste every inch of you and then you are going to suck my tongue again and taste yourself." His hand cupped my breast and his thumb pushed the lace aside freeing my swollen nipple. I watched as his head bent and he took my nipple into his mouth, sucking hard and swirling his tongue round and round, driving me insane. He nipped his way from one breast to the other and increased the suction as my panting grew.

I felt his hand caress the curves down the path to my ass and his hand grabbed my ass pinching hard, leaving me at the crossroads of pleasure and pain. He moved his hand to my front, finding my lace panties already wet. He rubbed the palm of his hand over the lace, up and down between my clit and my entrance. The friction built with each firm stroke, but not enough to allow my release. His fingers slipped under the lace and his thumb teased my clit in gentle circles. I needed more pressure. I arched my back to lean up to him and a low moan escaped. I shut my eyes and took a deep breath, "More" was all I could say, but he understood.

Kennedy increased the pressure, massaging my clit with rhythmic circles. Then he slipped a finger inside me and commanded, "Open your eyes, Hope, I want to watch you cum." I opened my eyes and they locked on his pale blue eyes and I felt my body begin to climax. I grabbed his shoulders and let it take over me. Pleasure rocketed through me and the intensity of my orgasm rippled in soft moans escaping my lips. I had forgotten that we were still standing and my knees began to buckle. Kennedy gently pushed me back and down onto the bed.

Before I could find words to speak, he kneeled at the side of the bed, and pulled me at the hips toward him. I was swollen and spent from my orgasm, but Kennedy's tongue touching my clit stirred something inside me. He gently used the flat of his tongue to lick my clit in long slow strokes. He circled the swollen nub firmly until I was on the verge of another orgasm and then pulled back. He blew on my clit lightly and then I was surprised to feel his tongue dive roughly into me. My body shivered and he again started with a steady aching rhythm, his tongue pulsing in and out of me quickly. My muscles tightened and orgasm pulsed through me in ferocious waves of pleasure. He let out a low growl and then licked and sucked until he swallowed every last drop of my cum.

He stood and undressed, never taking his eyes off of me. I gasped as he pulled down his boxer briefs, freeing his long, thick, erect cock. He gently laid his body over mine, his forearms on both sides of my face supporting his weight. He looked into my eyes, "All I could think about was making you cum all week Hope." His knee pushed my legs open making room for him. I could feel his erection at my opening. "You taste so sweet, Hope. I want you to taste yourself." His mouth devoured mine and I felt dizzy from his kiss. He pressed his cock into my opening and slowly moved, stretching my tunnel a little and pulling back out. Then he was back inside, further this time. "Jesus Hope, you are so tight." I swallowed hard at his words.

He took his time with short slow strokes until I was stretched wider and he was finally buried inside me. He grabbed the back of my knees and pulled my legs up to deepen his thrusts. I hadn't thought it was possible for him to reach any deeper. He looked down at me while he pumped harder and ground his hips slightly from side to side with each stroke down. His face was taught and his eyes seared into me. He took my mouth smothering my moan and another small orgasm washed over me. I felt the muscles in his back tense as he fiercely pumped into me. His thrusts slowed and I thought I heard him quietly whisper my name as he shifted his weight from me.

A few minutes later we lay tangled in each other quietly, our breathing returning to normal. "Hope, how long has it been since you last had sex?"

"Ummm…two years" I said with a shaky voice, honest, but embarrassed by my own admission.

He pulled his face out of my neck to look directly in my eyes and my answer was rewarded with the smile. The full on pearly white teeth with full deep dimples smile that would forever be seared into my brain. He said nothing more, but gave me a sweet kiss on the lips and got up and walked to the bathroom.

I heard the water running from the bathroom and thought perhaps Kennedy had decided to shower.

I was suddenly exhausted and raw emotion began to seep in as my brain finally caught up to my body. It has been so long since I was with a man, I wasn't sure what the proper etiquette was. Do I get dressed and leave? I grabbed my shirt and began to cover myself when Kennedy emerged from the bathroom. "What are you doing Hope?"

Startled at his question, "I...I...thought I should get dressed."

"Why? Do you want to spend time with me, Hope?"

He walked to the bed.

"Yes."

"Why?" His arms crossed, he struggled waiting for my response.

"Ummm."

"Remember our deal, Hope. No lies"

"Because you are the most gorgeous man I have ever laid eyes on and from the moment I saw you I haven't been able to stop thinking about you." Holy shit. Did I really just blabber that out? Immediately, I felt the blush move up my face.

Dead silence as he stared at me and I fought to stare back at him. "Jesus, Hope, you have no idea do you?" He approached and scooped me into his arms,

"We are taking a bath. You must be sore and I want to take care of you."

The penthouse suite bathroom was larger than my apartment. Floor to ceiling white marble and an enormous jacuzzi tub that looked large enough to hold six people. Kennedy placed me in the tub and positioned himself behind me cradling me between his legs. He washed my body slowly from behind and gently stroked the cloth over my swollen sex. I had never had a man wash me before and found the act intimate, yet soothing. After a long soak and the water had already begun to cool, he lifted me out and dried us both off.

"You must be hungry, would you like to go out to eat or order something in?"

I wasn't ready to let the outside world in and leave the cocoon that we had made together. "Order in."

Kennedy went out to the living room and I heard him on the phone. I looked around for something comfortable to wear, ruling out my work clothes lying in a pile on the side of the bed. Instead, I opted for Kennedy's dress shirt, which hung almost to my knees.

I went to join Kennedy in the living room. He stood at the mantle, next to the unlit fireplace and turned as I walked in. I watched as his eyes did a slow assault, taking in my half naked body in his partially buttoned shirt. "If you wore that to work, there would be a few years wait for a room here."

I laughed and went to stand in front of him. Without my customary four inch heels on, Kennedy had to be close to a foot taller than my five foot four self. I reached out and put my arms around him, just as his cell phone rang. He took a deep breath and breathed out a heavy sigh "I'm sorry, I should probably get this. I sort of left unexpectedly today and people may be wondering where I am. My CFO will send out a search party if he can't reach me for a few hours."

"Jenner" he answered the phone back to all business. "No, I apologize, I should have called earlier. I won't be able to make it tonight." I could hear a woman's voice ranting on the other end, even though the cell phone was pressed against his ear. But Kennedy made no attempt to move away for privacy. He pulled me closer to his chest, wrapping one arm firmly around my waist. He listened on the phone for a while but I didn't feel comfortable looking up to see the expression on his face. "As I said, I was wrong for not calling earlier, but something urgent came up. This isn't a good time to have this discussion, but I won't be free on any Fridays anymore." The voice on the other end got louder. He stirred, but his arm around my back only tightened as I attempted to pull away and give him space. "I need to hang up; I'm in the middle of something important I need to get back to Mikayla." Then he closed the phone, tossed it on the couch, and his other arm snaked its way around me.

I looked up, unsure of how I should react. Kennedy stared down at me, apprehensive. "It's over. My past isn't as wholesome as yours. Let's not go there." I gave him a small smile and nodded. The apprehensiveness slowly withdrew from his face. Both his hands cupped my face as he bent and lightly kissed the tip of my nose.

After we ate, Kennedy lit the fire and we settled in on the couch. My body ached and exhaustion swept over me. Kennedy pulled me back to lie down. My back tightly to his front and his hands covered mine. We stared quietly at the fire and I could feel my breathing slow. "Stay with me this weekend Hope."

My heart fluttered. "Ok."

***

The next morning I woke and leaned back to where Kennedy had been only to find the space empty and cold. I wandered through the suite and found Kennedy in a small office, which now looked like command central. He was typing on his laptop, the printer was printing and a fax was coming in. His cell phone buzzed and I wondered if this was what it was like for him always.

"Good morning sleepy head." Kennedy smiled up at me as I stood in the doorway.

"What time is it?" I didn't remember falling asleep but it felt like it hadn't been that long ago.

"7:30"

"In the morning? It's Saturday, don't you sleep in?" I did my best to look rightfully appalled.

"7:30 is sleeping in for me. I've been working for two hours already." A slight chuckle accompanied an amused smile. "Don't tell me you didn't Google me and find out I was a workaholic."

I wasn't sure if I should look embarrassed because I hadn't thought to research him or embarrassed because I couldn't comprehend being as alert as Kennedy already was so early on a Saturday morning. He took in my face and sat back into his chair. "You really don't know anything about me, do you?"

I searched his face and thought for a moment. "I know you gave me three orgasms yesterday and have good taste in art?"

"Come here Hope." I stepped in front of him and he pulled me into his lap. He pressed his cheek against mine and wrapped his arms around me tightly in an embrace. We stayed that way for a few minutes. He pulled back slightly so I could see him. "I want to take you out to my favorite restaurant tonight. I need to do a few hours of work. I've made arrangements for Charles to take you to the spa and shopping. I have an open account at the stores he will take you to and I want you to get whatever you want. Buy something new for dinner. Buy the whole store if it makes you happy."

"That's very sweet of you Kennedy, but it's not necessary. I can go home and get some clothes and come back later."

"Please Hope. I want to take care of you this weekend. Let me. You can have Charles pick up your friend if you want. Go enjoy yourself and then you are mine tonight."

***

Shauna's response to my invite via text was immediate. *Shut the fuck up. LOL. Of course I am coming. How soon can you be here?*

We spent the morning at the spa, being "Mr. Jenner's special guests" and then headed off shopping. Stepping out of the limousine in front of the exclusive boutique after a full morning of pampering, I felt like I was in a fairy tale. Shauna told Charles we were going to go for a short walk around the block before heading into the boutique and we made plans for him to pick up in two hours. Linking my arm to hers, we started off for a leisurely stroll. I knew she wanted to grill me. She was the best friend I could ever have and would like Kennedy if I did or give him a piece of her mind if he did anything to hurt me.

"So, the Adonis is back and you look like you have been well fucked." Shauna could talk trash with the best of men.

I told her all about the night and even shared the news of my three orgasms. "He is so sweet Shauna, I get the feeling he wants people to think he is all business and bossy, but underneath that ridiculously gorgeous exterior, he has a big heart."

"Well, the business and bossy part I've read about. I did some research this morning and I think you need to be careful. I mean, I want you to have a great time, enjoy yourself, but don't fall head over heels. Kennedy Jenner has a reputation of being a shrewd business man and always having a model dangling from his arm. All I'm saying is just know what you are getting yourself into."

Her words blew and I felt like the wind was knocked out of me. Obviously he is a bit bossy and I would have expected the shrewd businessman part, based upon his success and wealth. And why wouldn't he be a ladies' man? The guy is talk, dark, wealthy and ridiculously gorgeous. Women probably throw themselves at him daily. The thought made my stomach sour.

"I know I should probably want to know more about him. But for some reason, I want to learn it from spending time with him. Old Hope would have probably already dug up all she could and ran as fast as she could from him. I'm not sure why, but I don't want to run from him."

***

Shauna and I had a great time shopping. I tried on a dozen beautiful dresses that probably cost more than I make in a year, and then I settled on a new dress I could afford. The emerald green dress I picked clung to my curves and I thought it was more Shauna than me, but the sales clerk and Shauna said I had to buy it and I knew fighting with Shauna over fashion was a losing battle. Shauna talked me into adding some sexy lingerie for underneath the dress tonight and even I thought that was a good idea.

The saleswoman tried to put the bill on "Mr. Jenner's account" but I refused and charged it on my visa, holding my breath that the charge wouldn't be declined. It would take me a few months to pay it off, but the dress made me feel sexy and I wanted to feel sexy for Kennedy tonight. Charles pulled up outside the boutique just as we were finishing at the counter and we giggled the whole ride back Shauna's apartment. I sat in a daze as we drove the rest of the way back to the hotel. There was no denying that I was couldn't wait to get back to see Kennedy.

***

After a long, hot shower I wrapped myself in one of the luxurious plush robes the hotel offered in all of the suites and quietly walked into the living room. Kennedy was standing at the tall window looking out at the incredible skyline as the sun began to fade and the buildings began to light up. Wearing only low hanging sweatpants, the muscles in his back rippled on his tan skin. As I walked up behind him, I loosened the ties to my robe and let it fall open. Wrapping my arms around him and pressing my damp naked front to his back, instantly made my sex swell and heart flutter. My intention was for the gesture to be sexy and teasing, but it felt more intimate and loving than I had expected.

His breath hissed as he exhaled deep at my touch, "We won't make it to the restaurant at all if you don't put some clothes on very, very quickly." I could hear the restraint in his voice.

I giggled, a little embarrassed at my forwardness, and he turned to face me. I wanted him to see me as sexy New Hope and not nervous old Hope. "I don't mind missing dinner." I said with a devilish smile on my face. Kennedy stared down at me and I could feel the pink on my face heat. I might be able to hide old Hope with my bold words, but my face deceived me. His eyes searched mine and I wasn't sure what answer he was looking for.

"I need to feed you to get your strength up for what I have planned for later." His lips covered mine for a kiss that was way too short and then he took a step back and pointed toward the bedroom. "A box came for you while you were in the shower. Why don't you go get ready, Charles will be here soon."

Confusion by who would deliver something to me at Kennedy's hotel room, helped me ignore the disappointment of being rejected. I studied the large box on the bed recognizing the name of the boutique we had visited in the afternoon. My heart fluttered as I untied the large bow and lifted the box to find every dress that I had tried on and rejected because of the price tag that afternoon. Before I could turn around, I heard his voice from the doorway. "You should know that I don't take no for an answer when I want something. Even if that want is to give you a gift." His voice was serious and I found his tenacity flattering.

    I waited a minute before turning around to face him. Old Hope would have insisted on returning the dresses and felt unworthy of such a lavish expense. Fighting my own innate reaction, I tried to think of how Shauna would handle such a situation. She was the type of woman that men lavished with gifts. Hoping he couldn't see through me, I forced a smile and turned to walk to him. "Thank you." I stood on my tippy toes and reached up and gently kissed his cheek. A slow smile spread across his face revealing the dimples and I had to steady myself when my knees went weak.

***

    I don't know exactly how long it took me to get ready after that, my brain was too busy reeling from what had transpired throughout the day to focus. I walked out from the bedroom and froze. Kennedy may have reached Adonis status in his business suit, but dressed in dark slacks and a simple grey sweater made my mouth water. The sweater slightly stretched across his broad shoulders, one word came to mind. Power.

I saw his eyes sweep slowly up and down my body taking in my new dress. His eyes were dark and his voice had a dangerous throatiness to it "Jesus Hope. Fuck." I felt his reaction seeping into my skin and the small hairs at the nape of my neck stood erect. He walked to me never taking his eyes off of mine, I heard him take a deep breath. "You are beautiful." With just a few simple words, I was wet with desire. He lowered his head and gently kissed my neck slightly below my ear. It sent shivers down my spine. I melted when he pulled me close and held me in a tight strong embrace. He pulled back and cleared his throat "Dinner, now." And off we went.

The conversation at dinner came easily and Kennedy laughed as I told him stories of Shauna and I growing up in rural Oregon. Most stories had the same theme. Shauna getting herself into trouble and me having to save her ass. I told him about my father being retired from the service and how he married the former Miss Oregon after my mother died when I was 11. He told me he was the oldest of three boys, but didn't share any stories about his childhood.

When our waitress came with the dessert cart, he promptly told her that we wouldn't be having dessert and requested the check. Leaning forward, I arched an eyebrow and asked "Are we going out for more ice cream instead." The wine at dinner had made me bold and the way Kennedy looked at me made me feel sexy.

His face turned serious and he leaned forward close enough that I could feel his breath, "No Hope, I'm eating you for dessert"

My face flushed and I realized that I was playing in his game and he had just turned the table on me. "I've been thinking about how your tongue stroked that ice cream all day and I'm going to pretend you are an ice cream cone and lick you until your cream melts in my mouth."

I closed my eyes feeling raw with emotion and desire. I wanted to dig my nails into his rock hard body and take him deep until there was no air left between us. I forced my eyes open, his face inches from mine. "Well why are we still sitting here then?"

Kennedy's head drew back and a devious smile lit his face. He stood and grabbed my hand bringing me to my feet. He led me out of the restaurant pulling me behind him so quickly I could barely keep up.

Later that night I fell asleep in his arms after he made good on his promise of having me for dessert and I reciprocated by treating myself to another ice cream cone. Only this time the cone was Kennedy.

***

I woke Sunday still in his arms and gently tilted my head up from his shoulder to glance a look at Kennedy sleeping. To my surprise, he was not sleeping. He was looking down at me and began to stroke my hair. "Good morning beautiful." I smiled thinking how incredible it would be to wake up to this site every day. He smiled back, but it wasn't the full on dimple smile. "I have to get ready for my flight back to Chicago soon." The thought of leaving the cocoon we created over the weekend, deflated whatever excitement I felt waking up in his arms. I straightened at his words.

"Okay." I couldn't think of anything else to say without showing how sad the thought of not seeing him really made me.

He stopped stroking my hair and I readied myself for what I thought would come next. "I can't stand the thought of you in this city walking around so innocently with every man following your ass with their eyes while I am all the way in Chicago." Shocked, I leaned up on my elbow to look at him.

"That isn't exactly what I thought you were going to say." A moment later the realization of his words hit me. "And I'm not innocent Mr. Jenner." I did my best to look annoyed and serious. Kennedy, oblivious to the attitude I was throwing his way, threw his head back laughing. He looked at me smiling and then his face turned serious.

"You really don't have any fucking idea, do you?"

"Idea of what, that you just insulted me by questioning my toughness?"

He looked at me with arched brows and a slight curve of his lip. "Sorry beautiful, you're tough as nails."

***

We had room service for breakfast and then Charles dropped me at my apartment on the way to take Kennedy to the airport. We didn't make plans for the future. I don't know why I was afraid to try to talk about what we had out loud, but for some reason I knew we had something. Kennedy walked me up the stairs to my front door and turned to face me. He cupped my face in his hands and pressed his lips firmly to mine. Then he looked down into my eyes for a minute and I wasn't sure if he was waiting for me to say something. But he reached down and gently kissed my nose and smiled. I went inside and ran to look at the window. He was already pulling away.

***

Although my muscles were already sore from my workout with Kennedy this weekend, I forced myself to go to meet Shauna at the gym. Luckily the gym was busy so Shauna couldn't give me the full interrogation. I popped in my headphones and spent almost an hour on the treadmill reliving the fantasy of the weekend. Shauna had apparently lost patience with waiting to hear about the weekend, because she pushed the stop button on my equipment the minute she was done. When I looked at her annoyed, she just smiled and said loudly "Are you going to tell me about your fuckathon weekend or what?" The guy next to me took his eyes off Shauna's ass long enough to look me over and give me a smile. Shauna definitely knew how to get what she wanted.

Back in my apartment, I told her about our easy conversation and him buying me all the dresses that I had tried on. She wanted details on our "sexcapades," but I only told her that he was a good lover. For once she didn't push until she got more out of me. We ordered Chinese food and she told me about her Saturday night date. Shauna had a top ten list of things that men had to be dumped for, no matter how much she liked them. The poor guy didn't stand a chance when he hit two of the top ten before they even ate dinner – asking her to put on her cheerleading uniform for him later and looking in a mirror during their first date.

We cleared the table after consuming more calories than we had burned off in two hours at the gym, and Shauna told me that she had dug a little deeper into Kennedy.

"I don't know if I want to learn about him from reading stories that people who don't really know him write for money with a goal to sell their story Shauna."

"I just want you to be careful, Hope. It's not just all the pictures with models. He might have some other issues. There is tragedy in is his past. It's different from your past Hope, but you should know more than anyone that you don't walk through fire without coming out with a few burns."

Her words hit me as if I was physically struck. My stomach clenched and my heart raced. I could feel the blood rush out of my face and pool at my feet.

Shauna looked at me and took two quick steps toward me and hugged me tight. She didn't let go until my breathing returned to normal. Some things just will never change. And Shauna and I taking care of each other is one of them.

When I walked back to the kitchen table after saying goodbye to Shauna later, I saw the folder on the table. I wanted so badly to look, but it just didn't feel right. If I was going to have any chance with Kennedy, I couldn't let old Hope have an arsenal of information she could obsess on to destroy us before we had a chance. I took the folder and put it in my nightstand to avoid temptation.

***

I was surprised not to hear from Kennedy on Sunday night after the weekend that we shared. I was sad and disappointed when I didn't hear from him on Monday or Tuesday either.

Chapter 8

Franklin Jenner was thirty, two years younger than his older brother Kennedy, but he acted like the older brother most of the time. When the family business was passed down from their late father, the brothers split it up and each took the helm in different segments. Franklin operated the shipping company, while Kennedy took the financial division and Garrett, the youngest brother, took the biomedical operations. Franklin did well with Jenner Shipping International, and lived a comfortable lifestyle. He didn't quadruple the business as Kennedy had done after taking over the finance operations, but it was still a multimillion dollar paycheck each year.

Franklin married his high school sweetheart at twenty one and was the very proud father of six year old Emily and three year old Joseph. After their parents died, Franklin took over the family tradition of hosting Tuesday night family dinner. Garret was out of town, so this week it was just Franklin and Jenner sitting on the balcony after dinner enjoying a glass of Hennessey.

"I saw Mikayla at the Children's Hospital Fundraiser this weekend. She said you were in New York on business again. And she sounded pissed off." Franklin sounded amused.

"It's over with Mikayla but she won't give it up." Kennedy emptied his glass.

"So what's up in New York? Anything you need a hand with."

Kennedy dragged his fingers through his hair and let out a deep breath. He needed to talk to someone. "I met a woman there a few weeks ago."

"You mean a real woman or a Mikayla prototype?"

"A real woman. One I can't seem to stop thinking about and is making me lose my mind trying to keep myself in control." Kennedy poured another two fingers into his glass and stared up at the sky looking for the answer.

"Holy. Shit. You met a real woman!" Franklin slapped Kennedy on the back playfully. "It's supposed to be a good thing when you can't stop thinking about a girl big brother. Why the long face?"

"All I want to do is talk to her and see her. It's killing me to keep my distance. I can't focus and I think my staff is hiding when they see me I'm so miserable." The stress on Kennedy's face was evident.

"Well, why are you keeping your distance then? Is she bad news?" Franklin knew his brother hadn't been in a real relationship in a long time, but he was pretty sure Kennedy was smart enough to know that keeping your distance in a new relationship wasn't normal.

Kennedy tossed back the second glass and turned focused on the sky. "No, she is an angel inside and gorgeous outside. And she has no idea that she is perfect."

"Well with that combination, you better not take too much time to figure out why you are keeping your distance, because you can bet there will be a line of guys behind you." Franklin stood and put his hand on his brother's shoulder, unaware that his dad did the same thing when giving his sons serious talks growing up. "Look, someday you are going to have to let someone in. I don't know if she is the one, but I do know that you won't find out if you don't ever try."

Kennedy stared in silence for a moment. "Thanks Franklin, I'll be in in a few minutes."

***

Franklin reminded Kennedy about his god daughter's ballet recital the following weekend as Kennedy said good night to the children.

***

Wednesday morning Kennedy awoke with a panic. His brother was right and he needed to do something before it was too late.

Chapter 9

This week's training area was in concierge. It was difficult for me to offer advice to wealthy tourists who wanted to see the best sites of the city, when I had only saw a handful of the biggest landmarks myself. Worse, I was sad and a little angry and today felt like I was being tortured by an onslaught of honeymooners that were all in love and holdings hands. I saw Charles enter the lobby from the corner of my eye and I think my heart may have stopped beating for a second. It took a minute to compose myself when I saw Dylan pointing my way from reception.

Charles smiled when he saw me and tipped his hat. "Ms. York, lovely to see you again. Mr. Jenner asked me to deliver this to you." Charles extended his hand carrying a large envelope.

"Thank you Charles."

"You're Welcome. I hope to see you on Friday. Have a good day, Ms. York." Another tip of the hat and Charles was on his way.

As I opened the envelope, I wondered if Kennedy was coming to the city again on Friday. The thought of him coming on random weekends and expecting me to be available for "sexcapades" in exchange for a few dresses made me sick to my stomach. Even gorgeous and wealthy wasn't worth weekend visits from a man who didn't think enough about me to call once or twice during the week. How could I have been so wrong about him?

Inside was a short note and another envelope. *Hope. I'm sorry I didn't call. I screwed up. I can't stop thinking about you. Please give me another chance. Come to the ballet with me in Chicago. Please? KJ.* The second envelope held a roundtrip first class ticket to Chicago leaving Friday evening.

***

Wednesday night I laid in bed feeling surrounded by a man that I had only known a few weeks. The erotic painting reminding me of our first night together sat leaning against the wall in my bedroom, waiting to be hung. His note and ticket in the kitchen where I sat and read it at least thirty times before forcing myself to go to bed. Shauna was right, I should have been more careful with Kennedy. The weekend had obviously meant more to me than him, and I should have known that it was just a fantasy. My brain had finally caught up to my heart. Men like Kennedy Jenner didn't do happily ever after with women like me.

I tossed and turned for a while. In my head I had ended it, but my heart still needed closure. I reached for my nightstand and took out the folder Shauna had given me, searching for answers. I opened the folder and studied the picture on top of Kennedy with a stunning brunette. She had to be at least six feet tall and the legs on display under her short skirt had to be as tall as me. My heart shrunk in my chest and my eyes filled with tears. I skimmed through the next few articles looking at the pictures and saw same woman in several shots.

The phone startled me and I jumped sending the folder flying on the bed, papers spilling out all over. I dreaded late night phone calls, they almost always delivered bad news. I answered hesitantly afraid of what the call would bring. "Hello."

"You weren't going to call me or come this weekend, were you?" Kennedy's voice made my heart immediately flutter and I felt a flash of relief and excitement.

"Ummm..no, I, I, guess I wasn't."

"If you don't get on that plane Friday evening, I'll be getting on one."

My heart fluttered, and a glimmer of hope lit deep within me. Nerves always brought out my sarcastic side. "Going to the Caribbean if I don't go to Chicago?"

Silence for a moment. "If you would rather go to the Caribbean than Chicago, that works for me." A long pause. "Hope, I don't know what is going on between us, but I'm going to find out. I fucked up not calling for a few days. I'm sorry. But this isn't ending here. I'm not good at begging, but I can find other, more creative ways, to make it up to you."

He had me just by telling that me he was coming after me if I didn't get on the plane, the rest was a bonus. "Okay."

"Okay?" He asked as if he really hadn't expected his speech to work.

"Yes, I'll be on the plane Friday." I rolled my eyes at myself and smiled.

"Thank you. I'll let you go to sleep, but you can be damn sure I'll be calling tomorrow."

I laughed. "That's good. Good Night Kennedy"

"Good night beautiful."

I hung up the phone and gathered Shauna's research back into the file without another peek. Whatever I was going to learn about Kennedy, was going to happen on my own.

***

Kennedy called the next night. And also sent a huge bunch of wild flowers with a box of hand dipped chocolate covered strawberries.

Friday came and went quickly as I finished my last day of training in concierge. Kennedy had arranged Charles to pick me up at work and bring me to the airport. The flight was uneventful but I was nervous and spent most of it fidgeting in my seat. The man next to me was very nice and had assumed I was a nervous flyer. We chatted for a while and he told me that he was also from New York and taking a weekend trip to visit his sister. If I hadn't been spending most of my waking hours thinking about Kennedy, I may have noticed the stranger was handsome.

I saw Kennedy as soon as I stepped through security. Our eyes locked and he gave me the full double dimples smile. I smiled back and said goodbye to the man I had just sat with on the flight. I saw Kennedy eye the man as he said "Maybe I'll see you on the flight back Hope." And then I was pulled into Kennedy's arms and his lips covered mine pressing hard.

When he broke the kiss, I looked up and smiled "Hi. That was a nice welcome."

"That was Hello. You'll be getting the welcome when we get home." Sinister in his husky voice.

My legs turned to jelly and I thought I might fall. *When we get home.* I liked the sounds of that. A lot.

***

I wasn't sure what to expect of Kennedy's apartment, but whatever I thought was thoroughly overshadowed by the real thing. The penthouse suite might conjure up images of luxury, but that didn't begin to describe it. At least five of my apartments could fit in the living room alone. An entire wall of floor to ceiling windows with a majestic view of downtown Chicago and the riverfront. An enormous stone fireplace and sleek modern furniture complimented the view.

I took a few steps toward the windows. "Your view is amazing."

"It doesn't hold a candle to the one I have now." He stared at me as I stared at the view.

I smiled. "Do I get the grand tour?"

"You can have whatever you want." He said it like he really meant it.

The tour included a dining room that seated twelve, three guest bedrooms, a kitchen that a chef would drool over, five bathrooms, an outdoor deck and ended in the enormous master suite.

Kennedy turned to face me and pulled me into a tight embrace. He nuzzled his head down into my hair. "Does this conclude the tour Mr. Jenner?"

"I'm surprised I didn't pull over on the way here, I've wanted nothing but to taste every inch of you since I saw you in the airport." He pulled back slightly to look at me. "I'll show you the rest tomorrow, I promise."

"The rest?" He started kissing my neck.

"One floor down is my private office." More kisses. "The ten below that are the corporate headquarters for my company."

I think my jaw may have dropped open. But Kennedy didn't seem to notice. He was busy licking the delicate skin behind my ear and unbuttoning my blouse.

***

Saturday morning Kennedy gave me the remainder of the tour. Although mostly empty, there were a few people working in the corporate offices. Most of them didn't seem surprised to see the boss walking around on a weekend, but I got the impression that they were surprised to see him walking around holding my hand.

Kennedy told me the ballet was casual, so I dressed in jeans, a form fitting red v-neck cashmere sweater and chocolate brown high heeled boots. I thought it was strange to go to a ballet dressed so casual, but I'd never been to Chicago and assumed it was just different than in New York.

Kennedy drove us to the theatre in his sleek black Mercedes, holding my hand throughout the drive. We parked and walked into a small theatre and took our seats in the back. I was bemused when the curtain opened and there stood four, six year old ballerinas dressed in pink two twos with tiaras and glitter wands. Kennedy took my hand in his and gave a slight squeeze. "Third ballerina from the left is my god daughter and niece Emily." He grinned down at me sheepishly, a boyish smile so contradictory to his striking masculine face. That was the exact moment I realized I was falling in love with Kennedy Jenner.

When we reached intermission, Kennedy guided me outside. "I don't usually stay for the whole performance, my brother and his wife usually meet me across the street at Calhoun's and we grab a bite to eat with Emily. They sit in the front row with all the other video crazed parents."

I reached up and touched his face and then put both palms flat on his chest. "You are a very surprising man, Kennedy."

He eyed me warily. "I hope that's a good thing."

I nodded and leaned up and kissed him on the lips. I kissed him softly, a silent way of assuring him it was a good thing. But he took over and quickly deepened the kiss in response to mine. We both smiled and he took my hand to guide me to the restaurant across the street. As I looked up I was startled by a woman staring at us with daggers from the front of the restaurant. I gripped his hand firmly as we crossed the street and her eyes never left us as we made our way to the door that she was still standing in front of.

"Mikayla" Kennedy nodded.

"Aren't you going to introduce me to your little friend, Kennedy?" She motioned to me but her eyes never left Kennedy's.

Kennedy pulled me closer to him and put his arm around my shoulders. "Sure, Mikayla. This is my girlfriend, Hope. Hope, this is Mikayla. It was nice to see you Mikayla. Enjoy your evening." There was no time for a handshake, because Kennedy put his hand on the small of back and guided me into the restaurant.

The hostess seated us at a table large enough for three more to join us, and Kennedy looked at me with stress glaring from his face. "I'm sorry about that."

I thought for a moment. "Is it over with you and her?"

"Yes." He spoke without hesitation.

It soothed me to hear him say it. "Okay then, what are we ordering, because you are going to need a lot of fuel for later if you are going to top the evening we had last night."

I watched his shoulders relax and he smiled a full double dimples smile at me. He shook his head "No clue." He looked down at the menu still smiling and shaking his head. "Absolutely no fucking clue."

***

Franklin Jenner was the spitting image of his brother minus four inches putting him at about five foot ten. He also had paler skin and lacked the deep dimples that made my knees week. His wife, Lauren was tall and thin with girl next door youthful looks and a smile that said she was truly happy. The little ballerina, Emily, had golden curls, pale blue eyes and obviously had inherited her mother's penchant to smile.

Although the news of meeting Kennedy's family was only sprung on me two hours ago, it appeared that Franklin, Lauren and Emily had less notice than I. Kennedy introduced us all and Emily immediately insisted on sitting between Uncle Kennedy and me.

"Hope, I can't tell you how happy I am to meet you. I've heard so much about you in the last few weeks from my brother." Kennedy talked about me? To his family? I had been nervous about meeting his family, but now I was excited to learn more about Kennedy from a different view.

I smiled. "It's nice to meet you too. I hope some of it was good."

He smiled and looked at his brother. "Every word."

"Uncle Kennedy, are you going to marry Hope?" From the mouths of babes.

Awkward silence for a moment. I hadn't been looking at him, not wanting to make the uncomfortable question worse around people I just met. But when I looked up, Franklin and Lauren were staring at Kennedy and Kennedy was staring at me. He waited for our eyes to lock before answering. "If I'm really lucky, Em."

Something in his voice was raw and I felt tears well up in my eyes. Lauren saw my face and smiled and threw me a lifeline. "Emily, you shouldn't ask questions about people's private lives, honey."

Emily took off her tiara and handed it to me. "Okay mommy. But Uncle Kennedy never brings girls with him, so I just thought that maybe he picked this one to marry. Hope, will you try on my tiara?"

I smiled at Emily and reached down for her to place the tiara on my head. "I'll tell you a secret Emily." I quieted my voice as if I was telling a secret, but still loud enough for the table to hear. "When I was about your age, my favorite game was to play princess. I had a favorite tiara too. I wore it everywhere I went. I still have it. It's in my apartment in New York. If you ever come up to New York, I will make us some tea and you can try on my tiara too."

We spent the next hour talking about New York City. It was clear that Kennedy was close with his brother and they made me feel welcome and comfortable. As we were saying our goodbyes, Lauren hugged me while Franklin and Kennedy were talking and confided in me quietly. "We have never met anyone that Kennedy has dated. It was really great to meet you. I know we don't know each other well, but I can see the way that he looks at you that he's crazy about you. Kennedy is difficult to break through to and will sometimes fight to keep you out. But the man that is on the other side, is a man worth fighting for, Hope."

***

The drive back to Kennedy's was short and we both laughed as he told stories about Emily. He clearly adored his niece, and that made my heart swell a little more. The evening had been perfect and I knew it was a big deal for Kennedy to take me to meet his family. He was letting me in and I wanted to be there.

As we entered his apartment, his cell phone rang. He pulled it out and growled. "I'm sorry, I have to take this. It's business." Kennedy barked on the phone and I could tell that something was wrong. He listened and asked questions for ten minutes and then gave orders and hung up the phone without saying goodbye. He was tense and it radiated from his face. I wasn't sure how he would react to my reaching out, but I needed to help sooth him.

He stood against the kitchen counter, his legs spread and arms crossed. I reached up and softly kissed his lips, surprising him by reaching down and cupping him in my hand. I freed the button of his jeans and slowly lowered the zipper. He stared down at me and held my eyes. I reached inside and wrapped my hand around him. He was instantly hard. His body's quick response aroused me and made me bold. I wasn't a stranger to taking a man on my knees, but it had never been something that aroused me, I did it for them. But with Kennedy, feeling control of his body aroused me and I couldn't wait to take him in my mouth.

I rubbed up and down the length of his hard cock and when his eyes closed, I sank to my knees. The floor was cold and hard, but it didn't cool my arousal. I gently licked the head of his cock, swirling my tongue around the width of the head until I heard him exhale harshly. I fluttered my tongue up and down his long length until I heard his breathing speed up. Another minute of teasing and then I held the base of his cock in my fist and took him deep in one long downward motion. Adding suction I felt him grow thicker in my mouth. His hands wrapped around the granite countertop edge with white knuckle strength. He reached down and wrapped his hands in my hair, desperate to take over the rhythm.

"Fuck Hope, Fuck." His hips began to gently thrust as I bobbed up and down. The head of his cock hit the back of my throat and I swallowed, taking him down deeper. He groaned, a deep sound of pleasure and agony. I loved that sound and that he was losing control at my touch.

His thrusts became stronger and his hands wound tightly in my hair stilling my head. He was taking over. I wanted to give him what he needed, to remove his stress. I took his long hard strokes until the root of his cock touched my lips. I cupped his balls in my hand, gently squeezing, feeling them tighten with my touch. "Hope, I'm going to cum." I felt his hands loosen his grip in my hair and he was drawing back to allow me to release him. His thrusts slowed. I wanted to finish him in my mouth. I reached up and grabbed his tense thighs with both hands, and bobbed my head taking over where his thrust left off. He groaned loud, a sound that came from deep within.

I felt his hot cum fill the back of my throat and I struggled to swallow it all. Three large bursts set my throat on fire, yet I continued to pump my fist at the base of his cock, drinking every last drop. His body shook and he mumbled something incoherently but I wasn't sure it was even words. He was still hard as I released him, which amazed me after such a fiery orgasm.

He pulled me to my feet and held me to his chest. His arms wrapped tightly and I rested my head to the side, my ear against his chest, listening to his heartbeat. Kennedy had given me what I needed tonight at dinner. I knew he cared about me and it was more than just great sex. I was happy to be able to give him what he needed to help him relax with me.

We made love twice more that night, and it was the first time that our encounter had felt more like making love and less like sex. The passion and need was still there, but there was something more.

Chapter 10

The next morning dawned and I awoke with mixed feelings. I was snuggled on Kennedy's chest and his arms were still wrapped around me. It felt so good and so right, but the reality of my flight in a couple of hours left me apprehensive. "I'll come to New York next weekend." His voice broke into my thoughts and I wasn't sure if Kennedy sensed my insecurity or if he was feeling his own.

I looked up at him and smiled. We seemed to be doing a good job at taking care of each other's needs now. "That would be great. Would you stay with me? My apartment is smaller than your bathroom but I'd rather be there than at my work."

"Whatever you want Hope." He kissed the top of my head gently and we laid there quietly for a few more minutes.

"I need to make a few quick business calls, but then I'd like to show you the city before your flight."

I nuzzled tighter not really wanting to do anything that didn't entail Kennedy not holding me tight, but I knew my thoughts were irrational. "Okay."

I took a shower and Kennedy went to his office to make his calls. I didn't know that he had called his assistant and had her purchase a ticket for the seat next to me on my return flight so that it would remain empty, instead of being filled by the handsome man that sat next to me on my inbound flight.

Chapter 11

Kennedy didn't want to let Hope go home. He wanted to keep her in Chicago and send a moving company to collect her things in New York and never let her out of his sight again. But he knew his thoughts were irrational. How could he want to be with a woman all the time when he had known her less than a month? He had never even let women sleep over in his apartment, now he was dreaming of moving Hope in. He threw himself into his work, attempting to keep himself so busy that he wouldn't have time to think about all the men staring at his woman a thousand miles away. It didn't work, he couldn't stop thinking about her.

They talked on the phone every day, but it wasn't enough. He knew that Hope was meeting Shauna for drinks after work Thursday evening and the thought of men lining up to buy them drinks and try to put their hands on Hope was too much to bare. He was the boss, he didn't have to wait till Friday to leave for New York, he could come and go as his wanted. So he packed his bags and headed for the airport late Thursday. He didn't tell Hope.

Kennedy arrived at 10:30 and knew Hope was still out with Shauna because she was going to call when she got home. Charles picked him up and drove him to Salt, where he knew they were planning on going. As he pulled up, he saw Shauna exit the club arm in arm with a man. His heart raced and he dreaded watching the door to see who would come out next. Would Hope be on another man's arm? The door opened and Hope walked out alone, but a man followed a short distance behind her. He watched as Shauna and Hope spoke and hugged and the two men exchanged fist bumps. Then Shauna walked back to the man and took his hands and began walking in one direction and Hope took two steps in the other. The man that had been following Hope stood in her way and she attempted to walk around him. He put his arm out grabbing her by the waist and she pushed against him hard in an attempt to get away.

Kennedy bounded out of the car and took two long strides and reached for the man's throat. The asshole released Hope and started choking. Hope turned. "Kennedy!"

"Hope, get in the car!" Kennedy's grip tightened and the man's face began to turn red.

"Oh my god, Kennedy, please let him go, he didn't hurt me." Kennedy's face was stone and I wasn't sure he heard me, even though I stood right next to him.

"Get in the fucking car." A command, not a request.

I did as I was told and watched as Kennedy released the man who fell backwards on the sidewalk clutching at his neck. Kennedy said something to the man and then got in the back of the limousine.

"What are you doing here?" I was confused at the sudden turn of events.

"I came to surprise you. What the fuck were you doing?" Steel faced he looked at me for an answer.

"I....I...Shauna hooked up with that guy's friend and I told him I wasn't interested. He left me alone at first. But I think he had too much to drink and it made him more persistent. I told Shauna I wanted to leave and the next thing I knew he was in front of me on the street." Tears welled in my eyes as the realization of what had happened struck me. Would things have gotten even more out of hand if Kennedy had not been there? I felt the tears spill over and sting my cheeks as I began to shake in the aftermath of it all.

Kennedy grabbed me and pulled me close, holding me tight. I buried my face in his chest and sobbed. My eyes streamed tears that blurred my vision. I heard a deep exhale and then "It's okay beautiful, I'm never going to let anything happened to you again."

I was still shaken when we arrived at my apartment. Kennedy held me close that night in my bed. It was the first time we had spent the night without having sex. He made me feel safe.

***

Kennedy insisted on walking me to work the next morning. We strolled hand in hand and I watched the women on the street turn their heads as Kennedy walked by. Wherever he went, women's eyes followed. The attention he received would normally make me uncomfortable, but he seemed oblivious to it all and only gave his attention to me. As we arrived outside of The Monet, I sensed his concern from last night.

"Are you going to be okay today Hope?"

"Yes, I'm good. But what will you do all day while I'm at work?" I maneuvered my apartment keys off my key ring and placed them in his hand.

"I brought my laptop and have some calls to make. I also need to go shopping." He smiled, a suspicious smile.

"Shop? You shop? That's my second favorite pastime…can't you wait till tomorrow to go shopping so I can go with you?" I smiled and knew he caught my innuendo.

"Second favorite?" One eyebrow arched and a slight crooked smile.

I pressed my lips to his firmly in a kiss and stood on my toes to come close to his ear. "Well it used to be my first favorite, but having you inside me has toppled shopping from its perch on top of my favorites list."

He groaned. "Fuck. You can't mention me being inside you and leave me all day. I'm getting a hard on standing here."

I smiled and pressed my lips to his one more time and left him standing there watching my ass sway as I walked through the door to work.

***

The second floor of The Monet held all of the banquet halls and some offices. There was a staircase from the grand main lobby that led to the main ballroom and my office was off to the right. Outside of my office I could see down into the lobby and I often stopped to watch the people coming and going from the lobby. Many people were dressed up and it wasn't uncommon to see a bride or men in tuxedos. Tonight I stepped out of my office door and looked down at the lobby and saw Kennedy waiting for me. As I reached the top of the stairs, our eyes locked. His eyes didn't leave me the entire walk down. I didn't need foreplay with this man, I was aroused at just the way he looked at me with his hungry eyes. The man was sex on a stick.

As I reached the main floor, I saw the hotel manager, George, approach Kennedy, completely obvious to our interlude. "Mr. Jenner, I didn't see your name on our VIP list, will you be joining us this evening." George was a nice man and ran a great hotel, but he wasn't the greatest at assessing body language.

"No George, I came to pick up my girlfriend." Kennedy smirked and continued to stare at me as he spoke, but George still didn't get it.

George turned to me and politely asked "Hope, will you please ring Mr. Jenner's girlfriend's room?"

I smiled at George and turned my head to Kennedy. "Sure. Mr. Jenner, anything I can do to assist you is my pleasure."

Kennedy arched his eyebrow, a wicked smile. "Anything?"

"You bet your ass Mr. Jenner." I smiled back.

I saw George's head snap to my attention at my response. But Kennedy had already grabbed my hand and pulled me toward him planting his lips on mine. George was still standing in the same spot with his mouth hanging open when I turned back to say goodnight.

When we reached the street, Kennedy turned to me. "So, if I wasn't here, what would you be doing tonight?"

"Well, I guess I'd go the gym for an hour, then go home and watch a scary movie with a big bowl of popcorn and then try to fall asleep but I'd be so afraid of every little noise I heard that it would take me two hours."

He looked at me to assess if I was serious then "Ok, that sounds good to me. Let's go grab a change of clothes. Will your gym give me a guest pass?"

I nodded and smiled and off we went.

***

I dressed in my nicest gym clothes. I had bought the outfit as part of "Operation New Hope" but never actually wore it. The top was black and pink lycra and was really only half a top. The bottom was solid black lycra and I knew that it showed off my curves.

I changed into my sexy gym outfit and pulled my hair back into a pony tail. Kennedy was waiting for me outside of the locker room. He was wearing a pair of black sweat shorts that hung low on his waste and a t-shirt that was tight across his wide frame. The sleeves were snug on his ample arms and I was pretty sure I was going to have him wear that outfit when we were in private.

He stood there staring at me and I could see his jaw working to control his temper. I stopped in front of him and he took one step forward, into my personal space. "Do you wear that to the gym all the time?"

I was secretly pleased with his jealousy. "No, I have lots of different outfits."

He put his hand on the small of my back which was exposed and led me into the gym. "Let's get this over with before I get myself arrested."

I went to the treadmill and Kennedy went to the weights. I watched him workout and move from one piece of equipment to another. He knew his way around the equipment and I could see that he had a routine he worked. I pretended I didn't notice most times, but I know he turned to check on me in between each set of reps.

As I was finishing up my run and began walking a cool down, I noticed one of the woman trainers I'd seen approach him. She asked him if he was new to the gym as he exercised and he was polite but far from engaging. He didn't stop his exercise to participate in the conversation. The woman was not deterred, she continued to stand next to him and pretend to be interested in his exercise. But I could see from the way she looked at him that she wasn't interested in him as a client.

I could have walked over to him and saved him, but I was enjoying watching him try to politely rebuff her. Instead, I walked over to the water fountain in front of the equipment where Kennedy was exercising and did an exaggerated bend down to the fountain while I took a very long drink with my ass aimed right in his face.

I turned and saw him staring at me, a slight smirk evident on his face. He shook his head at me and I raised an eyebrow in response. The woman was still talking to him and didn't even notice he wasn't paying attention. Time for the big guns. I walked over to one of the bulking male trainers and asked about the times of the yoga classes for the night. Before he could respond, Kennedy had left the woman in the middle of her sentence and he grabbed hold of my elbow redirecting me toward the locker room.

I looked up at him with exaggerated big surprised eyes. "Oh, did you finish your conversation with your new friend already honey?"

Kennedy put his mouth next to my ear and whispered as we walked. "Very cute, but now I'm horny and jealous and I'm not so sure you will like the combination when we get home." As we reached the locker rooms, he smacked me on the ass hard. "Go change."

Outside the gym, Kennedy grabbed my hand and began walking so fast towards my apartment that I could barely keep up. "Are we late for something or are you just trying to use the walk home as some last minute exercise?" I wasn't sure it was smart to poke a bear that was hungry with a sarcasm stick, but I did it anyway.

He stopped abruptly and pulled me close to him. "When we get home I'm going to fuck you so hard you won't be able to walk back to the gym to see that steroid freak for a week."

His harsh words and jealousy were a complete turn on. When we reached the bottom of the stairs, I stopped and he tugged at me to hurry up. I looked at him shyly, "Umm, maybe we should walk around the block a few more times to properly cool down."

One step toward me and then I was up and tossed over his shoulder. He raced up the stairs. I laughed and hit his back with my flailing arms, but it didn't lessen his speed. He put me down just inside the doorway and closed the door. He turned me to face the door. "Hands on the door Hope." I did as I was commanded.

I placed both hands of the door and turned to look back at him. "Don't turn around." I felt his lips on the back of my neck as he began his way down my shoulder and back. He bit down on the sensitive flesh between my neck and shoulder. I gasped.

His hands pulled down my jeans and panties in one swift motion. "I'm going to finger fuck you, but your punishment is that you are not allowed to move. Every time you move, your ass gets another smack. Do you understand me, Hope?"

I nodded, unable to speak. I was so completely turned on, I thought I might come before he even entered me. "Bend over for me Hope, keep your hands on the door and don't let go."

I did as I was told. His long fingers circled my clit and I was unaware that I had even began to move to the rhythm he created until I felt the sting on my ass as his hand collided with my right cheek. I froze and then he continued. He put two strong fingers on my clit and added pressure to his circles. I moaned but stood perfectly still as he continued with his slow rhythmic torture. When I was on the edge, he slid two fingers inside me and pumped twice forcefully. Again, my body reacted to his touch and I wasn't even aware that I was moving until I felt the sting of his hand on my ass.

The pain coupled with his now pumping fingers inside me was almost too much to bare. I needed more. I purposefully circled my hips as I reached the edge and then his firm smack sent me over the edge. I moaned his name as I came hard.

"Jesus, Hope. You are so fucking sexy, I almost came watching you come." I heard his zipper go down and then he was inside me. He gripped my waist hard and he filled me with one hard stroke until I felt his balls slam against my clit. He pulled out and then another hard full stroke slamming inside me. I came again hard and pushed back and forth on him forcing him into and out of me as I screamed in ecstasy. I had never orgasmed that hard or that long in my life.

My orgasm sent Kennedy into overdrive. He pumped into me hard and fast gripping my hips and pinning me into place. With one last deep thrust he emptied himself inside of me with a guttural moan and I felt him shiver.

We both dropped to the floor and he held me, our labored breathing slowing together. "Jesus Hope, you have no idea what you do to me."

I smiled through my post orgasmic haze. "Well, I know what you just did to me and it was incredible."

***

Saturday morning we sat in bed reading the paper together and drinking coffee. It felt so simple and so right to start our day together. Kennedy asked if I could come to Chicago the following weekend to attend a charity event that his family supported. I asked about the charity and he told me that the charity provided funding for counseling for the siblings and parents of child crime victims. He explained that there are a lot of charities to help the victims, but few that helped get the families of victims counseling to learn to deal with their grief and the victim's grief. I smiled and said it sounded like a very thoughtful and worthwhile cause and that I would love to attend with him.

Charles picked us up for our afternoon of shopping and Kennedy wouldn't tell me what we were shopping for. Our first stop was to a police supply store. I was confused but played along. Inside, he spoke with the sales clerk while I walked around and looked at some of the uniforms. When the clerk disappeared into the back, I approached Kennedy. "Handcuffs?" I smirked and looked up at him.

"Nope." His face amused at my guess.

"Police uniform and burglar costume?"

"Nope, but that's not a bad idea...you see any sexy police woman skirts and tight shirts?"

I smiled and shook my head.

The sales clerk came back to where we were standing. "Do you know how to use it properly?"

"No, she needs a lesson." Kennedy motioned to me.

The sales clerk proceeded to give me a robust lesson on the do's and don'ts of using mace. When she was done and Kennedy had paid for three small cans of mace and a nice pink leather carrier, we exited the store. Outside, I stopped him and looked up with a serious face. "Thank you, it means a lot to me that you want to make sure I am safe."

"Beautiful, I'm not letting anything happen to you ever."

***

The next stop on our shopping trip was to the sporting goods store. Inside Kennedy picked out and purchased me five new gym outfits. They were pretty, but the tops covered my full front and some of my ass. I didn't fight him on the new outfits because he told me he either bought me new exercise clothes or he bought my gym and turned it into a woman only gym. I laughed at his threat, but I wasn't quite positive he wouldn't go through with it if I hadn't accepted the clothes.

***

I'd started to dread waking up on Sunday mornings, knowing that we would only have a few hours left before he would be gone again. We had a great few days and I didn't want it to end. I was starting to realize that I never wanted it to end. I stood quietly with my coffee thinking while I stared out the window.

"What are you thinking about." His voice startled me, I thought he was sleeping.

"Ummm." Crap, think of something fast Hope, you can't tell him that you are falling madly in love with him and want to make little Kennedy dimpled babies..."

He interrupted my thoughts. "Remember our deal Hope."

Damn it, I knew if I tried to lie now, my face would betray me. "I was thinking I hate when you leave." There, that didn't sound as scary.

Deafening silence for a moment, then he came to stand behind me. He wrapped his arms around my waist and looked out the window with me for a moment. "I've wanted nothing but to be with you since the moment I saw you." He turned me around to face him. Slowly he ran the tips of his fingers down my cheek, stopping to push an escaped lock of hair behind my ear. He kissed me gently. "I haven't had a girlfriend since I was 15 Hope."

His words confused me. I had met his last girlfriend in person and Shauna had told me she read a lot about him being a playboy. He saw the confusion on my face. "I guess you could say I dated. I definitely had a lot of sex and went nice places with women. But they were more arrangements; there was never any emotional attachment. "

I searched his beautiful pale eyes and saw truth. Then I threw myself at him. I couldn't help myself and I really didn't want to try. I jumped up and wrapped my arms and legs around him and squeezed as tight as I could. I never wanted to let go of this man. He laughed and hugged me back so tight I could barely breathe. I pulled my face back to kiss his face. I smiled and looked into his eyes. "That was everything I needed to hear." I crinkled my nose. "Minus the "a lot of sex" part."

We both laughed hard and we wound up spending the rest of the morning in bed. I still hated when he had to leave, but the memory of the day left me better prepared for the week without him.

Chapter 12

Shauna and I went out for dinner on Tuesday night to our favorite Mexican restaurant and I filled her in on my weekend. She told me about a new player that joined her team in a trade, and how she was hoping to make a trade of her own with him soon.

"So are you going to invite Mr. Wonderful to piss-ant Oregon to meet Mr. Hotty and his nasty ass bride?" Shauna had named my dad Mr. Hotty ten years ago when we got drunk for the first time down at the lake and she grossly admitted to me that she thought my FATHER was cute. As for his bride, nasty ass was one of the tamer names she had for the woman.

"I don't know, I'm afraid if I go back with him to Oregon, I'll turn into Old Hope and he will realize that I am not the person he thinks I am and take off running for the hills."

"That statement requires another margarita." She gulped down what was left in her glass and literally grabbed our waiter as he passed by. "We need two more margaritas quick." She batted her eyelashes to the poor nineteen year old waiter who was putty in her hands. Then she released her grip on his waist to go fetch them for her.

I felt my phone vibrate and looked down to check my texts. Kennedy wasn't a big texter, but if I was at work or out with Shauna he would send a text, rather than call. It was one of the things that I adored about him. *Charles will be outside in an hour and will wait until whenever you are ready. I don't want you ladies walking home in the dark after drinks. K.*

"Now, where were we? I'm going to say this once and for all Hope Marie York. And you better get it through that thick skull of yours. You are gorgeous, inside and out. That piece of shit step monster of yours was jealous of you all those years, that's why she always put you down. Do NOT let that little lying cheating bitch win. Kennedy wants you, not Old Hope or New Hope – just you!"

We looked at each other seriously for a moment, and then proceeded to crack up for the next five minutes. The combination of margaritas and Shauna trying to be the adult in our twosome made her lecture seem hysterical.

***

Charles pulled up outside of Shauna's apartment and she gave me a hug. "I could really get used to having a limo drive us around after a night of drinking." She winked and I watched as Charles walked her to the door. I saw Charles watching her swaying ass as it disappeared into the elevator.

Chapter 13

"So how are things between you and Hope going?" Franklin asked almost as soon as dinner was on the table.

"Hope? Is she cute? Does she have a friend for me?" Garrett was the youngest of the three Jenner brothers and made no attempt to hide his confirmed bachelorhood. At twenty seven he was named number two on Chicago's most eligible bachelor list this year. The notoriety caused a lot of family teasing but Garrett didn't care. He bragged he kept extra copies around and let them slip on the floor if a woman was initially resistant to his boyish charms.

Kennedy deadpanned to his brother. "You will go nowhere near Hope or any of her friends."

Garrett whistled. "Oh boy, big brother's got it bad, doesn't he?" He smiled to Franklin.

Franklin smiled back. "If you met this one Garrett, you'd understand. As beautiful on the inside as on the out."

Garrett pushed his luck. "I don't care what they look like on the inside, but I do care what they taste like on the inside." He raised and lowered his eyebrows a few times and smiled widely revealing smaller versions of his big brother's sexy dimples.

Kennedy ran his fingers through his hair and looked to Franklin for support, completely ignoring Garrett. "It's driving me crazy that she is so far away. Last week I watched some drunk asshole put his hands on her and I nearly lost my mind. "

"So move her out here." Franklin shrugged his shoulders like it was a simple solution.

Garrett arched an eyebrow at his brother. "Are you in love with her?"

Words weren't necessary. Garrett and Franklin smiled and watched Kennedy toss his drink back and blow out a deep breath. How had he not realized that he had fallen in love with Hope until now?

Chapter 14

Wednesday morning I was halfway to work when I started to have the feeling that someone was watching me. It wasn't the first time that I had felt it lately. Today it just seemed closer. I looked around as I quickened my pace and saw a typical New York City morning. Masses of people walking in all directions at twice the speed that people moved back in Oregon. People alone with headphones, people talking on the phone, cars trying to turn while people filled the walkway. I scanned the crowd again when I reached the final block to work and slowed to really look at the people around me. No one in particular seemed to be watching me.

Now that I was done training on the general hotel positions, my days were caught up in event planning. Most days I spent half the day meeting with potential new clients who were interested in planning an event at The Monet, and the other half working on planning events that had been booked. Today I spent the morning with a woman that I had vaguely recognized from the society pages, who was interested in booking her daughter's first birthday in the Grand Ballroom. While it was great for business, I had to wonder what the woman would do for the little girl's second or third birthday to top such an exaggerated first party. Lunchtime came quickly and I decided to have lunch in the park before making my way over to Park Avenue for an afternoon meeting with a party planner I would be working with on an upcoming charity event held at The Monet.

The leaves in the park were almost all on the ground and the ground was filled with vibrant autumn color. Deep orange and reds lined the path though the park and I decided to sit on a park bench close to the dog park. I loved to watch the owners interact with their dogs when they thought no one was looking. I wasn't sure if it was the feeling of being watched this morning, seeing dogs run around in an open area, or the beautiful fall colors that made me want to call my dad to check in. We hadn't spoken in a while and I knew that he was expecting me home for Thanksgiving.

"Hi Candace, is my dad around?" I knew she hated it when I called her Candace. Everyone else called her Candy. To me, Candy was a woman in five inch stilettos wearing blue tassels on her nipples as she danced around the stripper pole. I thought Candace was a beautiful name, but I had once overheard her tell someone that Candace made her sound old. Ever since that day, she was Candace to me. I couldn't overtly disparage her without hurting daddy, so I had come to enjoy the little things I could silently do to bother her.

He must have been sitting within hearing distance, because her feigned excitement and bubbly questions were certainly not a performance she would put on for just me. Dad and I talked about Thanksgiving, one of his service buddies retiring and Coy, my golden retriever. I told Dad that I met someone and was considering asking him to come home with me for Thanksgiving, and he gave me the third degree, but sounded pleased. I didn't mention that he lived in Chicago and we had been traveling back and forth,   I knew it would only make him worry more.

Dad and I had been through a lot together since my mom died in a car accident so many years ago. We both protected each other from things that would worry the other as much as we could. That was why I never told him about how Candace treated me after he found about her affair.

I was 15 the day that I saw Candace walking with the young football coach from his car into a house on Maiden Lane. She saw me too, but I didn't realize it at the time. I was young, innocent and trusting, so the thought never crossed my mind that she could be doing anything wrong. I guess I just assumed she was discussing something about cheerleading, since both of her girls were hoping to make the cheer squad and follow in their mother's footsteps from cheer captain to beauty queen.

Dad didn't flinch when I mentioned I saw Candace with Coach Fitzsimmons that afternoon, and it wouldn't be until two months later that I'd learn the truth while I eavesdropped on their argument one night. All of the years in the service had trained Dad well. He knew when to dig around when something didn't sit right with him. After my innocent comment, Dad had begun to follow Candace and found out she was having an affair with the young high school football coach.

For months after that, they fought a lot. But in the end, they decided to stay together and work it out. She blamed him for working too much and not giving her the attention she needed. He blamed her for breaking their vows and climbing into another man's bed. I didn't think any one man had the time or strength to give Candace the attention she thought she needed. But Dad had been through enough and who was I to judge.

After a year or so, they went back to normal and the fights about Coach seemed fewer and further between. Dad had begun to forgive her, but I'd already realized that Candace would never forgive me. I know down deep he forgave Candace because he didn't want to be alone again. He didn't want to experience the loss he felt when mom died. But Candace blamed me for their problems, because I was the one who first told Dad about the affair. She never believed that I acted innocently; she thought I wanted to sabotage her marriage. Life became hell for me at home at 15.

Candace had always favored her two daughters, but she was polite and friendly before. After the Coach incident, she began her verbal assaults on me. Her brand of cruelty may not have been physical, but it was no less scaring. At a time when girls needed their mother most, I was inflicted with relentless assaults of how ugly and unwanted I was and that I would never find a man.

I didn't tell dad and she didn't do it in front of him. At least not overtly. By the time it was unbearable to be in my own house with her, Dad was starting to heal from the torture she had put him through and I couldn't bear to see him hurt again. So I took it all, and after a while, she convinced me her words were true. If it weren't for Shauna, I don't know how I would have gotten through those years. She was my light in the darkness and the best friend anyone could have.

"So does this Kennedy have a last name?" I thought about making one up, because I knew he would be calling a buddy to run a background check that afternoon if I didn't.

"His last name is Jenner Dad, but please don't send all your buddies on a mission to find dirt."

"Now would I do that baby girl?" Yes, dad you most certainly would.

"Okay dad, I have to get going back to work now. Be good and I'll see you on the Wednesday before Thanksgiving."

"I love you baby girl." I could hear him sigh through the phone. He missed me and I knew it.

"I love you too Dad."

Chapter 15

Kennedy surprised me with a new dress for the Charity event we were going to Saturday night. "Did you really pick this out all by yourself? It is the most beautiful dress I have ever seen." The dress was obviously antique couture. The style was far removed from the harsh angles and lines of the current art deco fashion and was instead designed to show beauty and grace. The entire dress was decorated in light shades of pearls and iridescent beads. It looked like something out of a 1920's flapper movie, without the over the top flapper fringe. The pearls were set in a way to give the appearance of lace and then the dark beading appeared to shadow the lace. It was dusty rose and something I would have never picked out for myself. The neckline was low, but had layers of sheer fabric that made it appear romantic instead of overly sexy.

"You are killing me Hope, do you think I can't pick out something beautiful?" He arched one eyebrow and I saw the hint of a smile beneath the pretense of his hurt feelings.

"I didn't mean that, it's just so unique and beautiful, you must have had to spend a lot of time looking."

He took a sip of his wine with that sexy mouth. "You are right, I did. You really have to keep your eyes open for something that unique and beautiful." I could tell he wasn't talking about the dress anymore and I flushed. This man has seen me naked and in some pretty compromising positions, yet his words could still make me blush like a school girl.

"Why don't I put it on for you?" I smiled a devious smile. I had already put on the lingerie I had purchased for this weekend and was feeling confident at what his reaction would be. I kept my eyes locked on his and slowly untied the long green silk robe I was wearing. I let it hang open for a minute so he can see a hint of lace, before shaking my shoulders a few times to cause the robe to slowly slip down my shoulders and form a puddle at my feet.

His eyes darkened and bore into me. My breasts were pushed up and barely contained by the nude colored lace half demi cup bra. On the bottom, I wore matching lace boy short panties that fit me like a second skin. My thin shapely legs were covered by thigh high sheer stockings with a ribbon of satin and lace at the top. When I saw the lingerie on display I knew it was the perfect mix of innocent and sexy that Kennedy would love. I stood there for a moment and watched him drink me in.

"You are fucking killing me Hope. I'm going to have to be near you all night knowing that you have that on underneath your dress."

I smiled innocently. "What this? You like it?"

He took two long strides and gripped my waist forcefully. "Or we can be late and I can rip it off of you and fuck you from behind with that innocent look on your face, so I can remember that instead." His lips covered mine and he took my bottom lip between his teeth and nipped hard.

Every time I thought I was the cat, I wound up being the mouse with this man. "Kennedy!! We can't, I just spent an hour fixing my hair and makeup and the dinner starts in half an hour! We will be hours late!" Although my words told him we couldn't, my body had already reacted to his and my clit was swollen and nipples taught and erect.

He took a cautious step back and took a deep breath. "Go. Put the dress on, before I change my mind and we don't leave here at all."

The dress was exquisite on its own, but it clung to my body like it was made to fit me. It made me feel special. I walked out into the living room and Kennedy was waiting. "You look breathtaking Hope." His reaction made me feel as if I was floating. He walked to me and held something in his hand. "Turn around beautiful."

He lifted my hair and clasped a delicate necklace gently around my neck. I saw my reflection in the mirror above the fireplace. A simple, beautiful, delicate platinum chain held a three carat round pale pink diamond, surrounded by two circles made of smaller encrusted sparking pink diamonds. Gorgeous. I turned and held my hand to the necklace. "It's beautiful Kennedy, just like the man that put it on me. Thank you."

***

The charity dinner was held at the Hotel Marimount, Chicago's version of The Monet. It was luxurious and had an old world charm. I spent the entire cocktail hour being introduced to people that all seemed to know Kennedy well. I had been nervous about not knowing anyone and thought I might be spending a lot of time standing at the bar by myself fidgeting with my phone. But Kennedy never left my side. His left hand was clasped tightly with my right. He only let go when necessary to greet people, then it found mine again immediately.

Kennedy excused us from the last group of people and grabbed us champagne as a waiter passed by. We stood to ourselves for a while, while Kennedy told me stories about some of the people that we had met. We laughed together like best friends that were sharing years of inside secrets. I was disappointed when they announced dinner was about to be served and we had to go to our assigned table in the main ballroom.

I was happy to see that we were sitting with Franklin and Lauren. There were two other couples seated at the table. One I knew had to be Garrett,

Kennedy's youngest brother, they looked so much alike. Kennedy introduced his brother and his brother introduced his date. The other couple at the table was Kennedy's CFO and his wife. Lauren insisted that I sit next to her and Kennedy sat on my other side. Lauren and I chatted easily and Kennedy spoke to Garret across the table. Nothing felt forced. It felt right being with his family.

We were halfway through dinner, when I spotted Mikayla. She would have been hard to miss. She wore a daringly short black dress and her mile long slim legs probably came up to my shoulders with her six inch stilettos. Her hair was pulled back tight from her face and her flawless skin was radiant. I saw her look at Kennedy, then she looked directly at me and smiled an evil smile and turned away. Lauren must have seen the whole exchange because she leaned in to me quietly and whispered, "Ignore her, don't let the past get in the way of your future Hope."

I took a deep breath and smiled and excused myself to go the ladies room. Lauren followed me. We didn't talk about Mikayla or Kennedy, but I knew that she was silently showing me support. She spoke to me like I was part of the family and I felt comfort in her familiarity. I touched up my lipstick and decided Lauren was right, I wasn't going to ruin the night with my insecurities.

After dinner, Kennedy and I danced together. He held me close and I could feel eyes on us. I caught some of the younger women staring with what I thought might be jealousy on their faces. Were some of these women people who Kennedy had "arrangements" with before me? Was I staring at a bevy of beautiful women that had slept with him? Jealousy and insecurity crept in even as he held me close. When the music stopped, he whispered in my ear. "I can't stop thinking about taking that dress off of you." I felt his breath on my neck and it sent goose bumps down my arms and legs. All it took was a few words and I had forgotten my jealousy.

When the dance ended, Garrett walked over and asked me for the next dance. I could see Kennedy's jaw tighten and he begrudgingly allowed me dance with his brother. Garrett held me tighter than someone who I had just met should while we danced. He was charming and handsome and while he clearly was aware of his charms, it came off as boyish confidence instead of arrogance for some reason. He looked at me while we danced. "So, you must be someone very special for Kennedy to bring you here."

I smiled, unsure if the statement required an actual response. "Umm..Thank you?"

He laughed. "You're welcome."

His statement was kind but I wasn't sure if his brother meant that Kennedy didn't bring women to events like this or if this particular event was important to Kennedy. I tucked the question in the back of my mind for later. Before the song had fully ended, Kennedy was already at our side. "Okay little brother, you've had your fun, get your ass back to your own date and hands off my woman." My woman? Sort of cavemanish, but I liked it anyway. I smiled at Garrett and shrugged my shoulders. He shook his head and laughed and walked away.

A few hours later, we were saying our goodbyes when an attractive older woman approached me. Kennedy had gone to get our coats and I was standing alone. The woman gently reached out and took my hand in hers. "I just wanted you to know how thrilled I am to see Kennedy happy my dear. I know he's dated over the years, but in the fifteen years since he started the foundation, he has never brought anyone here. I know Kelly would be happy...wherever she is." She smiled at me with tears in her eyes and gave me a gentle hug. I smiled back, and felt, rather than saw, Kennedy return to my side.

"Kennedy, as always, thank you for your generosity to the foundation." The woman reached up and put her hand on his check. She turned to me. "You take good care of him my dear." Then she walked away.

Kennedy held my coat for me to put on and then lead me to the valet with his hand on my lower back.
We stepped outside into the cool air and I almost froze when I saw Mikayla standing there. A dazzling smile on her face she ignored me completely. "Kennedy, how wonderful to see you."

Kennedy nodded his head curtly, "Mikayla." His tone a warning. I felt his grip tighten on my back and he moved to stand closer to me. No other words were spoken and we waited in uncomfortable silence for our car.

We were both quiet on the ride home. I had so many questions to ask but I wanted to be able to see his face when he answered them. He poured himself something into a crystal tumbler and handed me a glass of wine. I watched him throw back the liquid in his glass in one long swallow. I resisted the urge to give in to my insecurities as long as I could. "Who's Kelly?" My voice just above a whisper.

Kennedy went to refill his glass. I watched as he loosened his tie and took off his jacket. He didn't turn to me when he spoke. "I don't want to talk about it Hope."

I stared at him from across the room, he didn't look my way. I needed reassurances and he wasn't going to give me any. He finished his second drink and placed the glass on the table. I watched him struggle with something. My heart started to pound and I wasn't sure what to do. I suddenly felt I should go home and sleep in my own bed tonight. But my bed was a thousand miles away and I had nowhere to run.

"I'm going to go to bed." I swallowed hard, fighting back tears.

I took my time in the bathroom and changed into my robe. I got into the empty bed and tried to relax myself with a few deep breaths. My head was spinning and I felt alone. I was exhausted but it still took a long time for sleep to find me.

***

I woke up the next morning and was relieved to find Kennedy asleep next to me. I watched him sleep and thought about the night before. We hadn't had a fight and he didn't actually do anything wrong. He had things he didn't want to talk about and that was okay. Everyone had issues and we didn't really know each other that long. Yet it still hurt.

We spent the day together and neither of us spoke about the night before. We cooked breakfast and lunch in our pajamas and I did my best not to think about Mikayla or Kelly or any other women that might have touched Kennedy. It was a nice day and we laughed a lot, but something was different.

Chapter 16

The next week we spoke every day, as if nothing weird had happened. I had known for the last two weeks that I wasn't going to see him this weekend, because he was flying to London on Thursday night for what he called an "overdue business trip." But after last weekend, it made it more difficult to not be with him.

Thursday afternoon my phone rang and I shut my office door when I saw his name on the screen. "Hey. This is a surprise, to what do I owe the pleasure of a mid day call from a busy executive."

"I can't stop thinking about you."

I smiled. "You're pretty hard to stop thinking about yourself Mr. Jenner."

"Come with me to London tonight." He was serious.

My stomach did a flip. "I'd love to, but I can't. I don't get any time off from work for the first three months."

His voice was low and edgy. "I can't wait another full week to see you Hope."

I hated the thought of not seeing him too. "Me too. But next week is Thanksgiving and I am flying to Oregon Wednesday night after work. I made the plans before I even moved to New York."

"Can I join you?" His voice turned gruff. "I need to be with you."

"I'd love that." I closed my eyes, excited at the thought of being with him in Oregon, but terrified of what he would see.

"I'll have Marcy make the arrangements." He exhaled audibly.

We talked a while longer and I told him about my plans to meet Shauna and her new basketball player for sushi Saturday night.

"Just the three of you?" I knew what he was asking.

"Shauna knows I am not interested in meeting anyone Kennedy."

"It isn't Shauna I am worried about."

A long pause. "Well you need to trust me Kennedy."

"I do trust you, it's the three million men in that city that I don't trust."

I laughed at his response, but he didn't. "Okay honey. I need to get back to work."

"Okay beautiful."

I disconnected and stared at my phone. His jealous tone had an edge that made my pulse speed up and heart thump faster against the wall of my chest.

***

Saturday night came and Charles dropped me uptown at the Japanese restaurant where I was meeting Shauna and her basketball player Jeremy. Kennedy had insisted that Charles drive me and wait while we had dinner so that I didn't take the subway uptown at night. I agreed because it made him feel better, but it also allowed me to wear the cutest pair of silver tie up Jimmy Choos that I had been dying to wear but were not made for subways.

Shauna jumped up and down with excitement when I entered the restaurant. Jeremy stood almost a good foot taller than her even though she was tall and wore heels. I saw another exceptionally tall man standing near Jeremy and Jeremy introduced him as his teammate Derek. I eyed Shauna angrily and she gave me a small smile and shrugged her shoulders as if to say, it wasn't her fault.

Dinner was delicious and the Saki helped me relax. Derek and Jeremy were both very nice and I managed to relax a bit and enjoy their company. We all laughed as Shauna told stories about the different ways she and her squad mates managed to sneak out after curfew when they were traveling for games. Derek and Jeremy didn't seem the least surprised when she told them that the fire drill the hotel had three nights ago was actually the product of a lot of flirting with the hotel manager when they found themselves unable to sneak back onto the floor due to team security.

When we exited the restaurant a few fans gathered asking Derek and Jeremy for autographs and I saw a few flashes from pictures. I called Charles and told him I was done and waited out front for him to pull around the block. Shauna hugged me and reminded me that tomorrow was pajama Sunday at my place and Derek put his arm around her around her and smiled at me. "She might be a little late." Shauna giggled.

As Charles pulled up Jeremy reached for my hand and politely reached down and kissed my cheek. "It was nice to meet you Jeremy."

He looked down at me. "Can I see you again?"

I smiled flattered. "I have a boyfriend."

He smiled back "Lucky bastard."

***

Sunday morning I awoke early to a pounding headache and ringing cell phone. "Good morning." My voice was still groggy. "What time is it there?"

Kennedy was awake and alert. "Two in the afternoon. Rough night?"

"Shauna and Saki. It's a deadly combination."

"I bet."

"Where are you?" I heard voices in the background.

"Trafalgar Square. I was in a meeting but needed to take a walk to clear my head."

"Everything okay?" He sounded stressed.

"I'm not sure. Why don't you tell me about your night? " My sleepy fog disappearing at his words.

I sat up. "You know I had plans to meet Shauna and Jeremy for dinner. I didn't know Jeremy was going to bring a friend."

He took a deep breath. "And."

"And we had dinner and then I went home, alone. But I'm sure you already knew that since I suspect you already spoke to Charles."

"I haven't spoken to Charles."

I was confused. "Then how did you know?"

He ignored my question. "Were you planning on telling me about your double date?"

I was annoyed at his insinuation. "It wasn't a double date, and if you hadn't called me accusing me of something, I would have told you. I don't have anything to hide."

I thought for a second. "And what were you doing last night Kennedy?" Maybe the reason that he didn't trust me had nothing to do with what I did last night.

"I had dinner with a seventy year old man and then went back to my hotel and went to sleep."

I didn't know what to say in response. We were both quiet for a moment. "I need to get back to my meeting. I'll call you tonight."

"Okay."

"And Hope, take a look at page 52 of the New York Daily." And then he hung up.

I got out of bed and went in search of ibuprofen and coffee. The New York Daily? Why did I need to read the Daily. I didn't read it often, although it was a popular paper, I thought they concentrated too much on sports.

***

By the time Shauna came over in her pajamas for our planned movie day at three, I was already three freakouts passed being freaked out. I remembered the precise moment the photo on page 52 must have been snapped. His large hand was wrapped around the top of my arm and he was leaning in and saying something to me while looking down and smiling. I was looking up and smiling. He had just told me that the guy I was dating was a lucky bastard, but the photo didn't make it look like we were discussing my boyfriend. It looked like they had captured us in an intimate exchange. No wonder Kennedy was so upset. The visual was bad. If the roles were reversed, and I was looking at a picture of him looking at a woman like that, I would have been just as upset.

"Well," Shauna did her best to find the bright side. "At least you look hot."

"Great." I gulped my water. "I'm sure Kennedy finds that very comforting right now."

Shauna knew what I was thinking. "If you think he's going to dump you over some silly picture, you haven't been paying attention to the way that man looks at you Hope."

"You didn't hear him, he was really pissed."

"He's 3,000 miles away and jealous." Shauna sat down on the couch. "You may not think so now, but this might actually be good for your relationship."

I looked at her like she was insane. "Sure, pictures of me smiling adoringly at another man will probably make him propose."

"A man like Kennedy struggles when he finds a woman like you. He isn't used to relationships and feels like he isn't supposed to want to be in one. At first he will fight it, but eventually he will realize he needs to stop fighting it and start fighting *for it.* The picture just helped him make the move to fighting for you."

I reached for her hand and squeezed it. I thought she was crazy, but I knew she meant well. "I hope you're right, because I'm in love with him Shauna."

She smiled confidently. "I know I'm right. And I knew you were in love with him before you did Hopeless." She bumped her shoulder into mine and called me one of the hundreds of nicknames that she had created over the years.

"So what are we watching today?" It was Shauna's turn to pick the movie, so I knew it was a b horror flick without asking.

"Evil Ranger." Shauna smiled. "It's about a park ranger that kills campers in the state park and blames it on wild bears."

"Sounds riveting."

***

It was almost nine before my phone rang and I was glad that he hadn't called while Shauna was still here. I didn't want to see the disappointment in her eyes if things didn't turn out according to her grand scheme.

"Hey." I said quietly into the phone.

"Hi." His voice was low.

I rehearsed what I was going to say to him in my head for the last hour, but the words were lost when I heard his voice. "I saw the paper, I'm so sorry. It wasn't what it looked like...not at all."

"Hope..." My stomach dropped as he said my name. I knew what was coming next. I loved this man, I had to try.

"Kennedy, he did ask me out, but I told him I had a boyfriend and then he said my boyfriend was a lucky bastard and they took that picture when I laughed at him calling you a lucky bastard because he didn't know

I was the lucky one and, and." I was rambling. "and I don't want to lose you over a picture of something that didn't mean anything to me but somebody made look like something and..."

"Hope." He interrupted me and I swallowed my thoughts. "I'm sorry." God no, he can't do this to me. He has to believe me. I waited for the rest of the speech. I knew what was coming... I'm sorry I don't want to see you anymore. He continued. "I'm sorry I accused you of something you didn't do."

He's sorry he accused me? Not sorry he was breaking up with me? I started to cry. "I'm sorry I stayed, I should have left when I saw Jeremy brought a friend."

"Fuck, Hope. Please don't cry. I was an asshole."

"I deserved it."

"No, you didn't. I'm sorry beautiful." His voice softened.

We talked for a while longer and when we hung up relief flooded over me. Is it possible Shauna was right?

Chapter 17

My flight to Chicago the day before Thanksgiving was early. We were meeting in the terminal and I couldn't wait to see Kennedy. So much had happened in the ten days we were apart and I was anxious to see if what I thought we had was still there. We had almost four hours before the flight to Oregon and our plan was to get some lunch and hang out in the executive lounge, where Kennedy was a member.

Two steps into the terminal from the gangplank and I saw him. He was standing at the counter and two attractive flight attendants were talking to him. I suddenly panicked. What if things were different? What if our fight and the time we spent apart had made things change? My heart raced and I could feel my knees tremble. He turned and saw me. The flight attendants didn't notice that they had lost his attention. Our eyes locked and he smiled at me. The bright full on dimples smile that stopped my heart the first time I saw him. He lifted me up and held me so tight I could barely breathe. Then he kissed me, right in front of the gawking flight attendants. Not a hello kiss, but a Hollywood movie kiss. The kind that makes fireworks go off in your head and people stop and stare wishing it was them. By the time we came up for air, I wasn't worried that things had changed anymore.

"Let's get out of here." His voice was gruff and sexy.

I smiled and shook my head. We took off through the airport in a sprint. I had no idea where we were going, but I wanted to get there with Kennedy. As we were about to go through security, I stopped, "Wait. Where are we going? We have to go through security again for our next flight."

"There is a hotel and conference center attached to the terminal. I'll order us room service in between fucking you the first time and making love to you the second." His eyes were dark with need.

One eyebrow arched, "We can eat on the flight to save time."

A crooked smile and one deep dimple. "That's my girl. Let's go."

***

We were barely inside the room when we began tearing off each other's clothes. I didn't want him, I needed him. I needed him inside me so badly it physically hurt. He unbuttoned only enough buttons on my blouse to reach my bra. He quickly pushed the silk back with his thumb and freed my nipples. He took one nipple into his mouth and sucked hard and then bit down before releasing it for the next one.

He lifted my skirt up and it bunched around my waist. One tug and he ripped my panties from my body. I gasped. His fingers quickly dove into my pussy. "Jesus Christ you're so wet for me already." He lifted me up and carried me over to the desk and cleared it with his free hand with one swoop. Everything fell to the floor. I finished unbuttoning his pants and freed him. He was hard as steel. I stroked the length of him and he let out a low groan. The sound was deep and erotic and my body reacted to just the sensation of his need.

He positioned me on the desk, the height of the tall desk aligned perfectly with his hips. His lips covered mine hard and I could feel the tip of his wide head against my clit. He turned his head slightly and deepened the kiss while his hips circled and then in one long stroke he buried himself until the root of his cock was pressed up against me. I whimpered with the pain of sudden fullness stretching me to my limit and my hands on his shoulders tightened, my nails digging into his back. He cursed under his breath and stayed planted deep inside me for a while before moving. His hands held my hips tightly in place and began pumping into me with a fury. I moaned and he sensed I was on the edge. "Look at me Hope, I want to watch you cum." I opened my eyes. His face was inches from mine. He looked so serious and beautiful as he stared into my eyes. My orgasm didn't have time to build, it hit square on like a ton of bricks. His strong hard strokes, his wanton need and his commanding voice were all too much. I moaned as it rolled over me. It felt so good I didn't want it to ever stop.

"Please don't stop, please, please." He moved with such strong rhythmic pumps that I didn't have time to recover from the first one when the second one rolled on top of the first. "Fuck Hope, I'm going to explode, I can't hold back." He came with a ferocious growl and I felt him arms tighten on my hips and then loosen with a tremble. He continued to thrust into me for a minute, but the thrusts softened and he found my mouth once again. He kissed me softly, tender and full of emotion. A tear escaped my eye before I could pull it back. He ended the kiss and rested his forehead against mine. Both of us still breathing ragged. I watched him follow the path of my tears down my face. He brushed the hair off my face and his thumb gently wiped the tears.

"Jesus, Hope." He studied my face and it made my heart do a flip. His emotions were on display on his face and he wasn't trying to hide them. It made my heart swell.

I smiled . "That was amazing. You are amazing."

He pulled me into his chest and squeezed me so tight it hurt. But I didn't care, I didn't want him to move an inch. He kissed my neck and I could feel his breaths slow down my back. We stayed that way a few minutes and then he pulled back and looked at me. "I need to feed you."

He ordered room service and when it arrived there was enough food for six. I looked at the food and then to him. "Umm, Kennedy, are you starving or something?"

He looked at the food confused for a moment. "Damn, my brain wasn't functioning yet when I ordered. I don't even remember ordering any of it."

We both laughed and then we ate too much and Kennedy kept his word and made love to me for round two.

**

We barely made it to our flight on time. I wasn't surprised when we boarded the plane that Kennedy had upgraded my ticket to first class. Aside from the fact that it must be difficult to fit his six foot two body in a regular seat, I'd already learned that when Kennedy bought things, he bought the best. As we entered the cabin the flight attendant did a double take when she saw Kennedy. "Good evening Mr. Jenner. We don't usually see you on this route. Can I take your coat?"

Always the gentleman when outside of the bedroom, he turned to me. "Hope, can I take your coat?" He handed both coats to the attractive woman. She did her best attempt at a smile, but seemed put off at having to take more than Kennedy's coat. She turned to me with a sugary fake smile "Oh, I didn't realize that you had an assistant joining you today."

Kennedy started to speak but I beat him to it. "The only assistant he has on this flight is you." I smiled back with all the sugar I could muster as I took his hand and we made our way to our seats.

When I finally noticed Kennedy was watching me, he held my eyes and leaned in. "That little attitude you threw just made me hard. What the hell are you doing to me?"

I smiled at him and arched one eyebrow. I didn't look away while I motioned for the flight attendant and spoke. "M'aam, may I have a white wine and Kennedy will have a Scotch, no ice."

Kennedy laughed and shook his head.

The flight was uneventful. Kennedy and I talked quietly for the first hour. He told me about his trip to London and the deal he was working on and I told him about Shauna's latest conquest. When the captain dimmed the cabin lights, I snuggled into him and he put his arm around me. I rested my head on his chest and his heartbeat soothed me as I lay there feeling warm, happy and content.

I must have dozed off for an hour, because the next thing I knew the captain was overhead asking the flight attendants to prepare for landing. "How was your nap, sleepy head?" He kissed my forehead tenderly.

I righted myself in my seat and started to think of the eminent visit with my dad and step mother. I was nervous about bringing Kennedy home and afraid being around Candace and her girls would tear any confidence I had developed to shreds as soon as I was back in their presence. Would Kennedy see what they saw when they looked at me? Kennedy saw New Hope and I didn't want to disappoint him when he discovered the real Old Hope.

I shifted in my chair, unable to relax at the realization of what was soon to come. "What are you nervous about beautiful?" He was already so good at reading me.

Luckily a good explanation came to mind. One that was not totally a lie. "Umm...I'm about to see my dad for the first time in three months and I have no underwear on and I'm afraid I look like I just had three hours of mindblowing sex."

"You look beautiful. Like the angel that you are. But every time I look at that skirt I remember you have no panties on and I picture that skirt bunched up around your waist. Your dad has a gun. I think I am the one that should be nervous."

***

"My house isn't exactly the luxury you grew up in Kennedy." I looked out the window as we drove through the small town of Florence. It was odd to be back home, even though I had only been gone four months. The houses all seemed so small and rundown now, although I had never noticed it when I lived here. New York was so filled with life and luxury, and it made the empty streets lined with small houses seem worlds away.

The homes were small but quaint, spread out between lawns that were now brown. The trees were already bare and summer flowers long gone. Driveways were made of rocks, not bricks, and were lined with old cars. A few houses had run down old cars on the laws between houses that looked like projects long forgotten. I wasn't sure if Kennedy didn't notice or if he just didn't mention it.

"I don't care if you grew up in a cardboard box, Hope. Besides, growing up with money isn't exactly what it's cracked up to be. My father was always at work and my mom was always out on the society or charity circuit playing a part. The size of a house doesn't really matter when it's always empty."

I had warned him that my Dad would be apprehensive about him. Being in the service had made him wary of people and it took him longer than most to offer trust to people's intentions. And, being that he was coming home with his only daughter, I expected my dad to be more apprehensive than usual. He would be polite, but he wouldn't get the same warmness that Dad reserved for me.

I told him a bit about Candace and her daughters, but I didn't tell him about how much she really hated me. I left him to assume that any tension between us was probably because of how close I was to my Dad and that she was my step mother. I wasn't ready to share the whole story of her years of torture and I might never be.

We pulled into the driveway and I looked at the house. Everything looked the same but yet it all felt so different. I didn't live there anymore. It was the first time I was going to be a guest in my house. I took a deep breath in and exhaled slowly. Dad walked through the front door and out onto the big white wraparound porch. He smiled at me. "You going to sit there and look at the house or you going to come in baby girl?" He took a swig of his beer, smiled and headed toward the car.

At fifty four, my dad could still pass for forty. Six feet tall and lean with an athletic body that he worked hard to maintain. He wore his usual jeans and t-shirt and his feet were bare. He had the start of some grey in his dark thick hair, which would soon turn into salt and pepper. Like me, he had green eyes and a pale complexion. He held himself like he was still in the service and had a naturally quiet demeanor that worked in his line of business because it kept people talking and allowed him to take it all in.

I hugged Dad and he lifted me up and spun me around. We'd been doing that dance since I could walk and I had forgotten how good it felt. I suddenly felt like a little girl again. Kennedy walked around the car and introduced himself, and the two shook hands. Kennedy caught me smiling looking at the two of them together and gave me a quiet smirk and head shake.

My momentary happiness came to a screeching halt when I walked in the door. Candace stood there eyeing me in between my dad and Kennedy with a murderous look on her face. She looked more glamorous than usual. Tall and thin with big blue eyes, a straight nose and mounds of well dyed blonde hair. Her lips were pink and pouty and her cheekbones were model high. She had a full, gleaming white smile that showed perfectly straight teeth when she turned her attention to Kennedy.   "You must be Hope's friend. Welcome to our home." He accepted her hand and I wasn't sure if Kennedy had noticed that his handshake was more contact than I had received from her.

Dad asked Kennedy what he was drinking and I was surprised when he told him beer. Dad brought me a glass of white wine and Candace requested water. We all stood around while dad and Kennedy talked about the flight and I watched as Candace eyed Kennedy. Her eyes studied him up and down and I was disgusted to see a look that said she liked what she saw, and not in a motherly sort of way.

After a while we all sat in the living room and I poured myself a second glass of wine. Kennedy seemed relaxed and comfortable and sat next to me on the couch with his arm casually around the back of my seat. His presence and the wine were helping me to relax me until Candace decided it was time for her interrogation to start. "So Kennedy, how did you two meet?"

"I was a guest at The Monet, the hotel where Hope works."

"A guest? Don't you live in the city?"

"Actually, I live in Chicago."

"Chicago? Well that must be difficult for a relationship."

"It's not the best situation, but we seem to have managed okay by taking turns flying on the weekends."

I felt dad's eyes on my face. I knew he wouldn't be happy with the idea of my traveling to Chicago all the time. "Kennedy picks me up at the airport in Chicago and has his driver take me to the airport in New York, Dad." I spoke directly to Dad, even though he had not asked a question. I knew from his face that he was concerned. He did his best at a small smile and nodded his head once.

"Well, that must get very expensive for you two to be traveling all the time." Candace wasn't going to give up until she founds something wrong.

"Candace….please." I felt the flush spread up my face.

"What, I'm just concerned for you?" Yeah right. Like there was ever a day where you had concern for anyone but yourself.

"It's okay Hope, I understand why she might be concerned. The truth is money isn't an issue. I have a successful business and a trust fund that will support my great grandchildren some day."

It was Candace's turn to turn pink. Only she wasn't embarrassed she was pissed. I knew exactly what she was thinking. Why would this gorgeous wealthy man be with me?

I turned to Kennedy. "You don't have to explain any more, I'm sure my Dad already knows more about your finances than I do." Kennedy looked at my Dad and met his gaze. Something seemed to pass between them, although no words were spoken. It was a male language that women were never taught. But I could tell Kennedy was okay with whatever Dad had told him.

***

Thanksgiving morning was a blur of cooking and cleaning up and Candace and I managed to work in the kitchen for hours with only a few snide comments thrown my way. Dad and Kennedy were in the den watching football when Ashley and Amanda made their grand appearance. I was busy stuffing the turkey when Candace ran to the door to greet them. I could hear her fussing about how beautiful they looked and how excited she was that they were home for the entire weekend from graduate school.

Ashley burst into the kitchen a few minutes later followed by Candace. They must have gone into the den to say hello to my Dad and met Kennedy. "Oh. My. God. Mom, why didn't you tell me that you were having a gorgeous man for Thanksgiving? I look a mess!"

"Are you talking about the guy sitting with Dad watching the game?" This was going to be fun.

"Umm...yeah, did you look at him?"

I smiled smugly. "I look at him all the time Ashley, that's my boyfriend." I had never actually called him my boyfriend out loud, but I liked the sound of it.

Ashley's mouth was actually hanging open. I looked at Candace who looked as if steam was about to shoot from her ears. "Close your mouth Ash, you might catch a fly." I smiled and twisted the tops off two beers to bring my men.

***

I think I caught both Ashley and Amanda drooling during dinner, and it wasn't at the sight of the twenty two pound golden turkey. I would have thought it would bother me that they overtly flirted with my boyfriend right in front of me, but it didn't. Kennedy showed no sign of interest in the beautiful twins. Instead, every time they did anything remotely disrespectful to me, I noticed he made a small gesture of affection toward me. A rub on my back, a brush of my hand, a smile only for me. I didn't know if he did it on purpose or not, but I felt like it wasn't just me against them anymore. Kennedy had my back. For the first time ever, I felt like I wasn't alone against them. And it felt good.

We made it through dinner, but by dessert I noticed that Candace had started to slur her words slightly. I wasn't counting, but I was pretty sure that she had three glasses of wine during dinner alone. The look on her face told me the alcohol was fueling a new fire about to roar. "So, Kennedy, do you want children?"

I nearly choked on the wine I was drinking. "Candace, I thought we were done with Kennedy's interrogation."

"It's okay Hope. Yes, I'd like children someday." He showed no fear as he responded to her.

"Won't that be difficult with all the traveling you do?"

He thought for a moment. "I've spent the last 10 years growing my company. To be honest, there was never anything important enough to keep me home. So when traveling was required, I did it. But I have built a great team now. I have people I can trust to take over some of the travel when my personal attention isn't required. I've already started to pass things off so that I can be home with Hope."

I saw another unspoken exchange between Dad and Kennedy. Their eyes caught and I saw Dad give Kennedy a small nod.

His answer was what every mother would want to hear. To know their daughter was being made a priority over work. But Candace wasn't looking for a mother's comfort. "Home? Which home would that be, New York or Chicago?"

"Right now home for me is wherever Hope is. We'll figure the rest out later." He looked at me and I smiled. He gave a slight smile back and raised one eyebrow silently asking if his responses were good. I stood to start to clear the table and leaned down to his ear and quietly whispered. "Perfect."

If I wasn't in love with him before, the way he handled Candace would have done it for me. As always, he was confident and in control. His manner was strong and powerful, yet he was respectful and dignified. I could understand why he was so successful in business. He was intimidating and well spoken and his presence controlled a room.

***

Our flight wasn't until late Saturday evening, and I had told Kennedy I wanted to go to the cemetery and visit my mom. I had never gone to the cemetery with anyone, except the day of the funeral. I went all the time; I just always wanted to go alone. Shauna and Dad had both offered dozens of times to go with me, but I'd always declined and they didn't push. But with Kennedy, he didn't offer to go with me, he was just going.

Dad had purposely picked a cemetery that I could walk to, since I was so young when she died. It was a long walk, but I had grown to enjoy it and never taken a car even after I learned to drive. Kennedy was dressed and ready when I got out of the shower. "I hope you don't mind, but I like to walk to the cemetery.

It's not a bad walk and I find it soothing on the way home."

"Not at all, you get ready and I'll meet you downstairs in a little while." He kissed my forehead and squeezed my shoulders before walking away.

It only takes Kennedy fifteen minutes to get ready and look like he walked off the cover of a magazine, but it took me at least an hour. I straightened my hair and put on light makeup. I chose a long flowing sand colored skirt with tall brown distressed leather boots. A cream tank top with a shaggy long fringed sweater and hoop earrings completed my so-ho gypsy look of the day.

I went downstairs and found Kennedy sitting on the porch with Dad. He had a beautiful bouquet of wildflowers that were tied up simply in natural cord. I knew they had to come from Gerlick Flowers just from looking at them. Gerlick was more of an artist than a florist, and I often went there to get flowers to bring to mom. If I had been in the store, those are the exact flowers I would have picked.

Dad stood and gave me a tight hug. Then he gave Kennedy a quick nod and put his hand on Kennedy's shoulder before walking away. Another unspoken exchange.

***

We walked to the cemetery hand in hand and Kennedy carried the flowers. We talked and laughed and recounted the last few days in Florence. "I think my step sisters have a crush on you."

He laughed.

"Have women always thrown themselves at you?
"

"Do you want an honest answer?"

"I'm not sure, do I?" I winced at the thought.

"It was great when I was young and stupid. But it gets old pretty fast."

"Aww....poor little rich pretty boy... sounds tough." I did my best fake sad face to feign understanding at the difficult time he must have had.

"Keep it up and I'll put you over my knee with that attitude. And I'll enjoy every fucking minute of it."

"You wouldn't dare."

He arched one eyebrow and smirked. "Try me. I've spent three days next to you and kept my hands to myself out of respect to your father. So you are already in trouble when we are finally alone. I'd love to spank that heart shaped ass of yours until it turns bright red."

I flushed. Jesus. The man can make my panties wet on the way to a cemetery! What the hell is wrong with me!

I bit my bottom lip to try to push the thought of his smacking my ass out of my head. It didn't work.

Kennedy gave me a devious smile and shook his head. "I can't wait to get you alone."

***

We visited my Mom's grave for a while. Dad had a bench placed in front of her headstone years ago, so that I could sit and talk to her. It was odd to share the bench with anyone. For years, I would sit and talk to Mom, telling her about what was going on in my life. Sometimes, when things got bad with Candace, I would cry and tell her how much I needed her and missed her.

"When she first died, I would come here and cry all the time. I didn't really know what to do when I visited. Then, as I got older, I would come here and tell her about my day or what was going on in my life. Sometimes I would cry and tell her it wasn't fair that I didn't have her anymore. Then, one day, I came for a visit and there was a funeral going on next to her stone. I watched from a distance as they lowered the small casket into the ground. It was a child. I came back a few weeks later and saw the headstone." I motioned at the headstone to my left. "Lilly was only 12 when she died and I watched her mother lay her to rest. After that, I came and told mom about my day, but I didn't complain or cry anymore. At least she got to live 35 years and have a child. Poor Lilly made me realize I needed to appreciate the time I had with her and stop living in the past in honor of Mom's death."

Kennedy didn't say anything. He put his arms around me and held me close and kissed the top of my head. When I stood and took his hand to leave, I watched as he opened the cord on the flowers and laid half at my Mom's headstone and the other half at Lilly's. He didn't know that I'd done the same thing a hundred times before.

***

We said goodbye and I promised to call next weekend. Dad reminded me that he was going to Connecticut for a conference in a few weeks and told me that he would love to see my apartment. He squeezed me into a bear hug and spun me around. I smiled and pretended I thought I was too old for him to still do that, but I actually loved it and he knew it. Kennedy and Dad shook hands. "You take good care of my baby girl."

Kennedy nodded. "I will."

"Candy says to tell you that she's sorry she got caught in traffic and won't get to say goodbye in person." I knew that Candace had purposely gone out to the stores a few hours ago and not come back in time to say good bye. But I was glad she at least made an excuse up so that Dad didn't feel bad.

Chapter 18

Kennedy was quiet the trip back to Chicago. I had a connecting flight to New York an hour later and I was secretly hoping that he would insist that I change my flight to Sunday, so we could spend the night together alone. He didn't. We sat together as I waited for my flight to get called for boarding, and he kissed me and held me tight before I boarded. I was a little disappointed, but I figured that he probably had a lot of work to do and I tried not to let my mind wander.

***

Kennedy woke in a cold sweat, his chest heaving with breath stolen by terror. He hadn't had the dream in four years. Why were they starting again? It took years of therapy for him to stop replaying the day Kelly disappeared in his dreams. He couldn't go through it all again. Not now. Not when he had found Hope. Hadn't ten years of living the same nightmare over and over been enough torture for his sins? He never remembered the beginning of the nightmare, but always woke up at the same part.

Kelly Preston had been his first love. They were 14 when they met. She was in his English class and he stared at her for a month before he asked her out. She had long blonde hair and drew pictures of angels flying over rainbows during class instead of taking notes. Her art was amazing and she couldn't focus when she had a picture in her head until she let it out on paper.

He asked her to the 9th grade dance in October and they were inseparable for the next 13 months. Every day after school they would walk hand in hand to the park. He would push her on the swing and she would jump off and fly through the air when she got high enough to launch herself. They spent hours every day sitting in the grass under the big oak tree and doing their homework until the sun set.

The summer of 9th grade she let him get to third base. By the beginning of 10th grade, Kennedy was already almost six feet tall and captain of the football and crew teams. Girls were starting to notice him. Kelly didn't like all the attention that he was getting and blamed him for encouraging the attention.

One afternoon, Kennedy was talking to Amber Maloney out on the field after football practice. He was dressed in his football uniform and Amber was dressed in her cheerleading uniform. He knew Amber liked him and she was a tease. They stood on the field and flirted for ten minutes after all the other players headed into the locker room. He didn't know that Kelly had come to meet him after practice and was watching them alone on the field from the bleachers.

Kelly ran home crying without letting him know she was there. But one of Kennedy's teammates saw her running from the field and told him she left crying. He went straight to her house after school, but Kelly's mom had told him that he needed to leave her alone, give her some space. She was upset with him and went to spend the night at her best friend Julia's house down the road.

Kennedy didn't go after Kelly. He listened to her mom and gave her some space because he felt guilty for making her upset again. He thought he would talk to her the next day, after she got it out of her system complaining about him to Julia. But Kelly never made it to Julia's house. No one knew that she was missing until the next morning when Kennedy went to Julia's to apologize. Julia hadn't even known that Kelly was planning on coming over until Kennedy told her the next day.

At first, the entire town searched day and night for her. Witnesses had seen a girl with her description get into a car with an older white man. Someone had even been able to recall the type of car and some of the letters on the license plate. A week later the car was found, but no one was in it. They had found Kelly's DNA in the car, and signs of a struggle. But after the car, the trail went cold.

The police spent six months working day and night on the case. Kennedy's family hired private investigators and brought in the best trackers in the country. They posted a large reward for information leading to Kelly's return. The reward uncovered all types of new leads, and all of them were tracked down. None led to Kelly.

On the five year anniversary of her disappearance, her family held a memorial service and the police moved her case from active to cold. Kennedy kept a full time private investigator on the case for five years after that.

His dream always ended the same.

Kelly was screaming and banging on the glass in the back of a car as it sped away. Kennedy was standing with Amber watching it pull away.

***

The next morning, Kennedy called Dr. Andrews. He hadn't spoken to his psychiatrist in more than four years, but he answered his call on the emergency number in two rings on a Sunday morning. "Dr. Andrews, it's Kennedy Jenner. I need to see you."

Dr. Andrews was out of town but they spoke on the phone for almost an hour and half and Kennedy told him about Hope and his nightmare. Then they made an appointment for Tuesday morning.

***

Shauna and I met at the salon for an afternoon of mani pedis before we headed to our favorite Greek restaurant. I couldn't wait to tell her about Thanksgiving back in Florence. "But I'm scared Shauna, I'm crazy in love with him, and sometimes I feel like he feels the same way….then other times I feel like we are on other sides of the Grand Canyon, even though he is sitting right next to me."

"Maybe he is scared too." Shauna closed her eyes and settled into the massage chair as the pedicurist painted her toes blood red.

"Have you met the man? He isn't scared of anything."

"Everyone is scared of something Hope. Why do you think he is such a successful business man? Because he doesn't show fear. But not showing fear and not having fear are two different things. You might be the man's kryptonite. I see the way he looks at you. That man loves you and you are probably the only one that isn't sure of it."

I sighed. "I hope you're right, because if he dumps me, you'll be the one eating ice cream out of the carton and watching depressing movies with me for three months."

***

Sunday night Kennedy called. We talked for a little while but he was quiet again. Too quiet. After we hung up I found myself feeling desperate and began analyzing the weekend I had thought went well over and over in my head. Did he think I was weak for putting up with Candace's behavior? Was I delusional to think he was falling in love with me too? How could I feel like he loved me one minute and that he is going to leave me the next? Maybe he felt badly about breaking up with me so quickly after I took him to meet my family and he was just going through the motions now to put some time between our trip and ending things.

Ugh! What am I doing? I had to force myself to stop thinking those thoughts. I turned the lights off to try to find sleep. I lied there for almost two more hours in the dark and finally fell asleep exhausted from fighting my own thoughts.

***

By midday Monday my nerves were getting the best of me. I hadn't slept well and too much caffeine had me on edge. I was glad that I had appointments all afternoon to keep me busy; it made the afternoon go by fairly quickly, although I kept my cell near me all afternoon hoping I would hear from Kennedy for no particular reason. He didn't call until late that night and our conversation was benign and short. I tried to dismiss the empty feeling I had by convincing myself he was busy with work after being away for so many days with me. But our conversation felt awkward and left me feeling like he called me just to be nice. The tone of his voice was almost somber, and I was convinced that we were headed down a path that would end with me shattered into a million little pieces.

Chapter 19

Dr. Andrew's office was simple and understated. Pale blue walls with two worn dark chocolate leather couches facing each other separated by a glass coffee table made the room feel warm and homey. An old oversized desk at the far corner of the room was covered with papers and files.

Kennedy spent two hours sitting across from the silver haired distinguished Psychologist. He had known Dr. Andrew's for almost fifteen years, but hadn't seen him in the last four. Kennedy told Dr. Andrews about the days leading up to the nightmare and his feelings for Hope.

"Our dreams often come from our subconscious and sort through memories we don't even realize exist in our brain. As we go through our normal daily activities, there are things that can trigger our memory. When we are awake, our psyche protects us and keeps us focused on the things going on outwardly around us. When we sleep, our brain can match the triggers to old memories and bring stored memories back into focus."

Kennedy had heard the speech before. He even understood what was happening before he spoke to Dr. Andrews. He didn't go to see him to understand the psychology behind his nightmares. He needed Dr. Andrews to tell him that it wasn't his fault that Kelly disappeared. But he knew why Dr. Andrews never told him that. Because it was his fault. If he hadn't been so selfish and made her cry again, she would never have run off. He made her run straight into the arms of danger and he didn't protect her. She trusted him and he let her down. She thought he would always be there to protect him, but he wasn't.

Dr. Andrews suggested that Kennedy tell Hope about Kelly, so that she could understand what he was going through. Kennedy said he would think about it, but he knew he could never tell her. He was ashamed to admit what he had done. Ashamed to tell her that it was his fault she never came home. That he didn't protect her enough.

***

Tuesday afternoon Kennedy sat in the large glass conference room at the head of the long conference room table. His executive team had just completed a monthly presentation on the status of their open projects. But he hadn't really heard a word that any of them said. He wasn't even sure how long he had been sitting there since the meeting had broken up. He couldn't stop thinking about Hope. He was consumed by her. Obsessed. What if something happened to her while he was Chicago and she was in New York? He wouldn't be able to live with himself if harm ever came to her. What could he do? There was only one answer. Dr. Andrew's was wrong, he didn't need to tell her about his past. He needed to make sure it didn't happen again. Hope needed to be safe.

He needed her to move to Chicago with him. The sooner the better.

Chapter 20

I was nervous about seeing Kennedy Friday night. He wasn't the kind of man that took the easy way out, so I knew he would break up with me to my face and not over the phone. I dreaded him coming almost as much as I couldn't wait to see him. I watched out the window until I saw Charles pull up outside and then I went to the door. Kennedy climbed out of the back seat and pulled his duffle bag onto his shoulder. He had come straight from the office and still had on slacks, a dress shirt, and jacket, although the tie had been replaced with a few open buttons of his crisp light blue shirt. I drank him in. My eyes couldn't help but slide all over him. He looked every inch the powerful businessman. I shuddered at the thought of losing him.

He came toward me, long fast strides dropping his bag at his feet as he stood in front of me. "Hope, is everything okay?" I nodded and I watched him search my face. His arm wrapped around my waist and he pulled me against him tightly. His focus on me was intense. A slight frown between his brows. "Hope, remember our deal."

Damn him. He didn't even have to say the word lie, and now my face would give me away if I even tried. My Dad had the same effect on me when I was fifteen and Shauna and I would come home late with excuses ready for his interrogation.

"Let's go inside." I couldn't lie, but at least I could stall or try to change the subject.

I watched as he shrugged off his jacket and sat at the table. He took my hand and pulled me onto his lap. "I've missed you." One hand reached under my skirt to rub the outside of my thigh while he spoke. "Now tell me what's bothering you."

I watched his hand through the fabric of my skirt, avoiding his eyes. "It's just been a long week." Which wasn't a lie, the days felt like months as I waited for the moment of reckoning to come.

His other hand lifted my chin, forcing me to look at him. "All right." But he didn't look convinced. His fingertips glided across my face, his eyes searching for more. The way he looked so concerned made my chest hurt. His blue eyes were warm and caring.

"Let me make you forget your week then." His hand under my skirt shifted from running up and down my outer thigh to lightly tracing the sensitive skin on my inner thigh. Kennedy could make me forget the week. He could make me forget everything that happened before he walked into my life. His thumb grazed the sensitive skin between my legs and I was instantly aroused.

I closed my eyes but could feel him watching me. My face was so close to his, I could feel his warm breath. He adjusted me in his lap to allow my legs to open wider. I reached for his shirt and he grabbed my hand and pulled it to his mouth, kissing each finger tenderly. "No touching, I'm making you forget your week angel." I let my head fall against his chest and relaxed into him.

His thumb rubbed my clit in small gentle circles. I felt the tension build inside me and my nipples hardened against the lace of my bra. My pulse quickened as his thumb pressure became stronger and the circles grew faster. A small moan escaped. He pulled my panties aside and pushed one finger into me, stroking slow and steady until I grew wetter. He slid a second finger in and I arched into his hand as he increased the rhythm. His thumb rubbed against my clit as he pushed his fingers in and out of me until I was close. He plunged a third finger into me and I was on the edge. His voice was deep and raspy, "Cum for me angel." And it was all I needed to tumble over the wall. I came with a whimper. "Look at me baby. I want to watch you cum." I opened my eyes and my eyes locked with his. I was unable to look away and he watched as the tears streamed down my face. "Fuck Hope."

I was still breathless as he pulled me close to him and held me tight. I sobbed into his shirt and he didn't let go until I'd let it all out. I pulled back from his embrace and looked at him. I didn't think about what I was going to say, it just came out. "I'm in love with you Kennedy. If you came here to break up with me, please just do it and get it over with."

He looked at me for a moment. He lifted me up and carried me to the bed without saying a word. Then he made love to me until we fell asleep exhausted tangled in each other.

***

My eyes fluttered open the next morning to find him watching me. "You're staring at me."

He brushed the backs of his fingers over my cheeks and kissed my lips gently. "Move in with me. Come to Chicago and move in with me." His eyes never left mine.

"What?" Not exactly what I was expecting.

"I can't handle you being so far away. I need you close to me." His face was serious.

"But, I just moved to New York and I have my job here and a lease on my apartment."

"I own a hotel in Chicago. You can be the event planner there if you want to work. And my attorneys will get you out of the lease here, or I'll buy it out if they can't."

I leaned up on my elbows. "You own a hotel in Chicago?"

"And one in Atlanta and one in Los Angeles."

I was excited to hear Kennedy tell me that he wanted me to move in with him, but something was missing. I'd told him I was in love with him last night, but he didn't say it back. Did he feel bad that he couldn't so this was his answer?

"Why do you want me to move to Chicago?" I really needed to know.

"I just told you Hope, I can't handle being so far away from you."

My head was spinning; of course I wanted to move to Chicago to be with Kennedy. I'd move anywhere he wanted me to go, but I needed to know that he wanted me to move for more reasons than he just didn't like me so far away.

"I need to think about it Kennedy. It's such a big change and I just want to make sure it's right for me."

"You love me right?" He stroked my cheek.

"I told you I did last night."

"Then what else is there to think about?" His fingers stroking my cheek stopped in their place. He looked silently at me, waiting for an answer.

I looked up at him. "A lot Kennedy. Yesterday I thought that you were coming here to break up with me. Sometimes I feel like I'm on a roller coaster. When we are together it all feels so perfect, yet when we are apart, I feel like I'm going to lose you."

He kissed my neck and whispered in my ear. "Then if we are together all the time, you won't feel that way anymore."

Although I loved his logic, I wasn't quite sure that it was the answer. I smiled up at him. "Give me a little while to think about it anyway, okay?"

His face grew pouty and I could tell that he didn't often not get his way. I put both hands around his neck and pulled his face close to mine. "Maybe you should spend the morning trying to convince me?" I arched one eyebrow provocatively and pulled the sheet out from between us so that our naked bodies were touching.

"Oh yeah? You keep looking at me like that and I'll convince you so good you won't be able to walk into The Monet on Monday to give your notice."

***

When Charles came to pick him up on Sunday evening, I wasn't ready to let him go. I wanted to tell him that I would move to Chicago, but something was holding me back. Instead, we said goodbye and I told him that I would come up to Chicago the following weekend. Maybe when I was there it would all fall into place?

Chapter 21

Thursday night was a "friends and family night" for Shauna's team and I had promised her that I would come to watch the game. All of the players and cheerleaders were given tickets and their guests were all seated in the luxury boxes and the team hosted a big party after the game. I'd gone last year and it had turned into a wild party by half time. At the end of the game, after all the fans left, all the players and cheerleaders joined in the party and it continued on the court floor. Shauna had made plans for me to go with a few of the guests of her friends on the squad, some of them I had met before and liked.

When I had told Kennedy about the night, I could tell from his voice that he wasn't thrilled, but he didn't try to tell me not to go. But I'd agreed to have Charles drive me home when it was over, and promised I'd call him when I got in.

There was about ten minutes left in the game when I decided to try to find a bathroom outside of the luxury box. I'd had a few beers and my bladder didn't have patience for whatever was going on inside the luxury box bathroom between the couple that I saw slip in a few minutes before. I was about to walk into the bathroom when I was abruptly stopped in my tracks by a long arm hooking around my waist.

"Where's your boyfriend tonight you bitch." Spoken with a drunken slur.

Startled, I looked up to find the guy that Kennedy had threatened after he grabbed my arm outside of Salt. He was drunk and angry.

"Let go of me." He laughed at my request and tightened his grip.

Then all of a sudden I was free and the guy was flying through the air. A very large scary looking bald guy, that looked like he was either a professional wrestler or just escaped from prison, had drunk guy by his throat up against the wall. My rescuer looked vaguely familiar, but I couldn't place why. "I'm sorry that happened Miss." I didn't have time to say thank you as I watched as large scary guy twisted drunk guys arm behind his back and escorted him down the hall.

The rest of the night was uneventful and I managed to relax a bit by the time Shauna arrived for the after game party on the court. We danced and drank and I almost forgot it was a weeknight when I looked at my watch and saw it was after 2am. I called Charles and he was outside waiting when we stumbled to the car laughing. He drove Shauna home and then I was back at my apartment.

My phone rang as I was undressing and I nearly fell over trying to climb out of my pants while running for the phone. "Hello"

"You were supposed to call me when you got in." I could tell he was annoyed.

"I just got in and was going to call you after I changed." I did my best to hide my slur.

"Tell me about your night."

The alcohol loosened my verbal filter and I found myself blabbering, telling him more than was necessary. I told him about the fight that broke out in the luxury booth when two women realized they were both invited by the same player they were sleeping with. I described how two of the players did backflips in the air while dancing and admitted that some jerk bothered me and a stranger stepped in and took care of it. I hadn't realized that I was doing all the talking and he wasn't as amused at my stories as I was.

"I should have taught that asshole a lesson the first time."

I started to say it wasn't a big deal when I realized I hadn't told him that the guy who bothered me was the same guy from the restaurant a few months back.

"How did you know who bothered me?" I was suddenly alert and sober.

Quiet for a moment. "I need to make sure you are safe Hope." There was no apology in his voice.

Holy shit! He has people following me? "What does that mean?"

"It means exactly what I said."

"You are having me followed?" My voice was suddenly loud and I was mad as hell. "You don't trust me?"

"It's not you that I don't trust Hope." His tone was stern. I felt like a child being scolded. How dare he?

"Is that why you want me to move to Chicago? So that you can keep a better watch on me?"

"Why don't we talk about it tomorrow when you get to Chicago, when you're sober and calm." His voice was patronizing.

"Because I won't be in Chicago tomorrow!" I was so angry I was panting. I had fought back all of my own insecurities and jealousy for this man and how did he repay my efforts?

"Don't do this Hope." He sounded as if I was the one that was insane.

My voice broke and cracked. "You have no idea how hard it is for me to trust people, and I gave you my trust. I thought I had yours in return. Without trust, we have nothing." I sucked in air and took a deep breath. "I need some time to think Kennedy."

I waited for a response from the other end of the phone, but nothing came.

"Good night Kennedy."

"I didn't mean to hurt you Hope."

I disconnected the phone and sobbed uncontrollably. I didn't understand what I had done to make him question my trust. Forgetting that it was 2am, I picked up the phone and called Shauna. She heard my voice and was at my apartment in less than a half an hour.

***

Shauna walked in and took one look at my tear-streaked face and was instantly ignited. "What did he do to you?"

I was rambling uncontrollably "Oh Shauna, I told him I loved him!" My hands were trembling.

"Oh sweetie, did he tell you he didn't love you?"

"No, he didn't say that. He asked me to move to Chicago."

"What? When? I don't understand. So why are you crying? Isn't it good that he wants you to move to Chicago?"

"No, he wants me to move because he doesn't trust me. He had me followed!"

"He said that?" Fury laced her words.

"Remember the guy who bothered me outside the restaurant a few months back that Kennedy threatened? Well, he grabbed me tonight and some guy stepped in."

"Why didn't you tell me that someone bothered you tonight?"

"I don't know, I didn't think it was a big deal. The guy was drunk and grabbed me and some guy I didn't know took care of it. It happened so quickly. But the guy I didn't know wasn't a stranger who stepped in. He works for Kennedy and he was following me because Kennedy doesn't trust me."

"How do you know that Kennedy doesn't trust you?"

"Why else would he have people following me? And whose side are you on? Are you sticking up for him?"

"I'm always on your side Hope, you know that. But maybe there is more to it than you think."

"It all makes sense now. Everything seems perfect when we are together, but then when we are apart things change. He asks me to move to Chicago, yet he doesn't love me. The puzzle didn't make sense until now. He doesn't trust me, it's why he is so different when we are apart." My voice cracked.

"Oh Hope." She pulled me into a tight hug until I calmed down. "If that's true, then he is a god damn idiot and doesn't deserve you."

***

I looked like death the next morning when I arrived at work barely on time. It made it easy for me to pretend I was sick and take the afternoon off. Dad was going to be in Connecticut for the weekend, and I had decided to get out of town and spend some time with him. An early start to a weekend with Dad was just what I needed. He was thrilled to hear I was going to spend the weekend with him, but I could hear the concern in his voice when I told him that I needed to get out of town to do some thinking.

Kennedy's picture popped up on my cell phone when it rang. I sent the call directly to voicemail. He didn't call back for the rest of the day and I didn't listen to his voicemail.

Dad and I had dinner in the hotel restaurant and then went for a walk. He hadn't mentioned Kennedy during dinner and neither did I. We stuck to safe topics and I told him all about my job and he caught me up on some of friends from the service.

We walked the first few blocks in silence. "So what's going on baby girl?"

I didn't even pretend to not know what he was talking about. I just told Dad what had happened with Kennedy and he listened. "Being in love isn't always easy princess."

"I know Dad, it's just that, you know, if he doesn't trust me now, where does it go from here?" I was choosing my words carefully, not wanting to hurt his feelings.

He took a deep breath. "It's difficult to have a relationship without trust, but sometimes when you love someone enough, you can work it out. You can give trust time to grow and develop. I'm not saying it's easy, but there are harder things to overcome."

I thought about his words, but didn't understand. "What is harder to overcome than a relationship with no trust Dad?"

He stopped and looked at me. "Losing the person all together, baby girl."

I was so deeply saddened by his words. "I'm sorry Dad, I know you loved Mom a lot."

"I still do sweetheart. And I don't know what you and Kennedy have together, but my guess is that man doesn't want to hurt you or not trust you. Sometimes people act because of their past and it has nothing to do with the person that is in their present. Maybe you should find out what makes the man who he is today."

Growing up, my dad didn't give me lectures or push his beliefs on me. Yet I always knew he was there for me with advice if I needed it. His advice was never the answer to my problem. Instead, he somehow always managed to guide me to the path to find the answer I was looking for myself.

I looked at him as we walked hand in hand. I held back the tears for his sake, but I couldn't get my voice louder than a whisper "Thanks Daddy."

A hesitant smile on his face. "I hope it works out the way your heart wants it to princess."

***

The next morning when my phone rang during breakfast with Dad, he watched me as I glimpsed at Kennedy's picture on the screen and then swallowed hard and answered. "Hi"

"Where are you? Are you okay?" It wasn't anger in his voice, it was something else.

"Yes, I'm fine. I'm having breakfast with my dad in Connecticut. I decided to get out of the city and come spend the weekend with him. I'm driving back in the morning."

"We need to talk."

I let out a deep breath. "I know. Why don't I call you when I get home tomorrow night, when I am back in the city."

"I'll be waiting."

After I put my cell phone away, I looked at Dad. He gave me a pensive smile and a quick nod of approval. I wasn't sure if he approved of Kennedy, but he was glad I was going to find out what was right for myself.

***

Dad insisted that I get a spa treatment while he was at his conference that afternoon. I hadn't realized how tense I was until my body started to relax half way through the one hour stress relief massage. My eyes closed and my muscles relaxed, I laid in the dark room quietly thinking after the treatment was over. How had I gotten here? I am completely and utterly in love with a man and I'm not even really sure what he feels for me. I felt scared and vulnerable. He could obliterate me with only a few words.   I was sure Kennedy had no clue how I was feeling. Scared and vulnerable weren't in him. Unlike me, he was strong and in control.

***

It felt odd to unpack clothes from my overnight bag and not have spent the weekend with Kennedy. We had spent every free moment we could find with each other since we met. I opened my dresser drawer to put away the t-shirt I had packed but never worn, and the ice cream painting Kennedy had bought me after our first date stared at me. My body reacted to the memory of our first date. The way he made the hair on the nape of my neck stand on edge with just a brush of his hand against my skin. I remembered how he looked at me, like I was the only woman in the room. Like no one else but me existed for him and we were in a secret universe. I missed him already and couldn't allow myself to think I had seen him for the last time.

It was a little after six when I finally managed to get up the courage to call him. I wasn't sure what I wanted to hear. He answered the phone on the second ring and my heart skipped a beat at the sound of his voice.

"Are you back home safely?"

"Yes. How was your weekend?"

"You weren't here, how do you think it was?" He didn't speak with sarcasm in his voice, but his words were decisive and factual.

"I'm so confused about what is going on with us Kennedy." My eyes closed and I sighed hating how weak I sounded.

"I didn't mean to upset you with putting a bodyguard on you. He wasn't supposed to interfere in your life; you shouldn't have even known he was around. I only want you to be safe beautiful."

I was irritated by his lack of apology. Did he think the problem was that the goon interfered with my life or that he had hired the goon at all? "I should have known he was around. If you wanted to put a tail on me I should have been involved in the decision."

"He wasn't a tail. He was there for your personal safety." His response was terse.

"And why would I need a bodyguard at all?" I could give attitude right back to him.

"I told you, for your safety." He was getting angry, but I was angrier.

"Well if he wasn't following me, and was only there for my personal safety, why didn't you tell me that you had hired him?"

"Because we would have had this fight sooner, rather than later." He was probably right, but the response just pissed me off even more.

"Why do you want me to move to Chicago Kennedy?"

Silence for a moment and then "Because I want to wake up to your beautiful face every day. I want your smile to be the first thing I see every morning when I wake up and the last thing I see every night before I fall asleep. Because my apartment seems empty without you in it, and it physically hurts to go through whole days without touching you. Because I haven't been able to focus since the day I met you, and I don't think I could live with myself if anything ever happened to you while you were in New York and I was here."

I was speechless. I don't know what I expected, but it wasn't that. "Wow. I don't know what to say."

"Say you forgive me and will move to Chicago Hope."

My heart told me to scream yes, but my brain hadn't gotten there yet. "How about if I say I forgive you, but I need more time to think about moving to Chicago?"

He let out a deep breath. "Okay, but I'll have to spend all of next weekend demonstrating the benefits of living here." His voice was sexy and sultry.

"Sounds like I just made a very good deal for myself with a hard core negotiator, Mr. Jenner." I flirted my response.

He laughed and I closed my eyes and envisioned him smiling the full on dimple smile that made my knees go weak.

"Actually, I'm the one who got the good deal Ms. York. I can think of nothing else I'd rather do with my time."

***

Monday and Tuesday went by quickly. The hotel manager, George, was on vacation so I was helping out the assistant manager that normally worked nights on some open projects. I was glad that we were so busy, because it kept me from counting the minutes until Friday night when I walked off the plane and got to see Kennedy.

Shauna was excited about Kennedy and I trying to work it out, and had decided that new lingerie was required for the upcoming weekend. She took me to Starlet's Palace downtown in Greenwich Village after work, and we spent almost two hours laughing and trying things on. From the outside of the store it appeared that they sold romantic lingerie, but the inside was anything but romantic. It was crammed with merchandise from floor to ceiling, and it was astounding to see that much sex related paraphernalia in one place.

There had to be hundreds of different vibrator choices alone, and then there was an entire side of the store dedicated just to fetishes. There were rubber suits, whips, chains, role play costumes, inflatable dolls, rows upon rows of sex toys ranging from nipple clamps to penis grips. The whole store was just too much to take in at once. The woman that worked there looked like the thirties version of the girl next door and was dressed in a catholic school uniform cut short enough so that her ass cheeks actually showed without bending.

I settled on a white lace bustier with emerald green ribbon lacing through the top and skimpy white lace panties with a hidden slit in the crotch for easy access and a G string in the back. The lingerie was displayed with a sexy lace garter belt and sheer white thigh high stockings. I added an emerald green garter and Shauna swore that the outfit was sex kitten meets librarian. We left the store $350 later, but I couldn't remember the last time I had giggled that much.

Later that night I pulled open my end table drawer to put away my purchases and saw the folder that Shauna had brought me when I had first met Kennedy. I had completely forgotten about her research, and the events of late had made me curious to find out more about Kennedy's past. Even my Dad had encouraged me to find out how Kennedy's past had shaped him into the man he had become.

I poured myself a glass of wine and set the folder on the bed. I wasn't really betraying Kennedy if I did a little research, was I? My head told me I wasn't, but for some reason my heart didn't agree. I knew I had to find a way to get my head and heart on the same page, and I wondered if the folder held some answers. I took a few sips of my wine and opened the folder hesitantly. The first few articles were from social pages and had pictures of Kennedy and different women. Some of the pictures were of Kennedy and Mikayla, others had pictures of women that I didn't recognize. But all were beautiful and the photos made my stomach go sour.

My attention caught on a picture of Kennedy and an older woman that I had met at the benefit we attended for families of victims in Chicago. The picture was a few years old and the woman was younger, but it was unmistakably her. I remembered she had told me that she was glad that Kennedy seemed happy and that Kelly would have been happy for him too. But Kennedy had never explained about Kelly so I scanned the article for an answer.

Erica Preston and Kennedy Jenner attended the fourth annual Families United charity event at Hotel Marimount. Mr. Jenner founded the organization to help cover the costs of treatment for surviving family members of victims of violent crimes. The organization was founded in honor of Kelly Preston, Mr. Jenner's high school sweetheart. Ms. Preston disappeared seven years ago, at the age of 15 while walking to a friend's home. The police investigation determined Ms. Preston was taken into a car against her will based upon blood found in an abandoned vehicle. Ms. Preston's body was never recovered. Families United provides assistance to families that have difficulty resuming their life after surviving tragic events.

My heart stopped and shattered into a million little pieces. I clutched my chest in physical pain. Kennedy. The man that I deeply love had loved and lost and my heart broke thinking of his hurt. I couldn't bear the thought of what he must have gone through. How it must have had such a profound effect on his life that it was still such a big part of him so many years later. My beloved strong and unwavering Kennedy.

I saw more of the puzzle pieces fall into place before my eyes. He was scared of something happening to me. He needed to protect me. He wasn't having me watched because he didn't trust me, it was to protect me. He had told me that from the beginning and I didn't believe him. Dad was right, the past had made the man who he was today. But why didn't he tell me? It would have been so easy to just explain. Did I even give him a chance to explain? I was such an idiot.

Chapter 22

I was glad to see George back at work on Wednesday, because I had decided the night before that I couldn't wait until Friday to see Kennedy. I told George I needed to take a few days off for a family emergency and booked a flight for that afternoon. I rushed through the morning of rescheduling appointments and taking care of things that had to be done before I left. I knew that it was risky to ask for time off when I had only been there a few months, but George seemed understanding and I had already decided that I was going whether I was allowed the time off or not. Luckily, it worked out and I still had a job when my flight landed at O'Hare late Wednesday afternoon.

I hadn't told Kennedy I was coming, because I wanted to surprise him. The last ten days had been difficult for both of us and I needed to see him in person. I called him in his office when I got into the taxi so that I could confirm where I was heading. I was relieved when he answered the phone so quickly.

"Is everything okay?" I didn't usually call him in the middle of the day.

His voice set me at ease. "Yes, I'm just having a busy day and wanted to hear your voice."

"I'm in a meeting right now. But that is good news. Can we pick this up in an hour?" It was evident that he had people sitting around him, but I could tell he was smiling when he spoke.

"Sure. Have fun at your meeting."

I dropped the phone into my bag and fidgeted in my seat. I was excited and hearing his voice made me feel tipsy, as if I had been drinking all morning. Twenty minutes later, I saw his building from a distance and took out my mirror to freshen up my makeup while we sat in traffic.

We pulled up and I felt like a little girl waking up on Christmas morning and seeing the tree lined with presents underneath. I opened the door of the taxi and my gaze went to the front door. Mikayla was walking out from the building and caught me in her sight as instantaneously as I had caught hers. She gave me a knowing smile and I watched her laugh at me from a distance.

I froze, unable to move either out of the taxi or back in. The impatient taxi driver interrupted my thoughts. "Miss, I can't double park here so you are going to have to get out now." My brain was trying to process what was happening. Why was Mikayla leaving Kennedy's office? Was she the appointment that he had to hang up on me for? I suddenly felt a wave of nausea come over me. Mikayla stood in front of the building watching me as I folded back into the taxi.

"Please take me back to the airport." My heart was pounding and I was sure I was going to vomit in the taxi. The thought of Kennedy with Mikayla made me sick to my stomach and the inside of the taxi was spinning. I was dizzy.

The driver shrugged and pulled away. "Whatever you want Miss, it's your fare."

I didn't cry the whole way back to New York. I just sat in my seat and went through the motions in a trance. I was numb.

***

I thought Kennedy might come to New York when I didn't respond to his messages on Wednesday night, but he didn't. Thursday I didn't get out of bed all day. My work had already given me the days off, and I was in no condition to function and plan other people's happy events for them. I knew I had to deal with Kennedy, but I didn't feel strong enough. I hadn't slept most of the night and woke myself up crying after two hours when I finally did fall asleep.

I was in and out of consciousness all day, alternating between crying and feeling sorry for myself and being angry with Kennedy. I was still wearing the clothes I had wore to work the day before when I answered the phone flashing Kennedy's picture.

"Hello." I was glad he had caught me when I was angry instead of crying. At least I could get away with some semblance of my dignity.

"Hey. What happened last night? I tried to call you back after my appointment, but it kept going to voicemail."

"After your appointment?" My voice was getting loud already. "How was your appointment anyway?"

"It was productive. What's going on Hope, you sound upset?" Upset didn't quite do enough to describe what I was feeling. Angry, betrayed, heartbroken, violent.

"I saw your appointment Kennedy."

"You saw Mark?"

I laughed with sarcasm. "Yeah right, Mark. I saw Mikayla leave your building."

"You are in Chicago?"

"I *was* in Chicago. And my timing was perfect. Mikayla and I had a conversation without words outside of your building. Then I realized I was a complete idiot and came back to New York."

"I don't know what you think you saw, but I haven't seen Mikayla since the night we both saw her at the charity dinner." His tone was curt, his anger evident.

"I can't do this anymore Kennedy. I was so worried that you didn't trust me that I didn't stop to think it was because you couldn't be trusted. I thought I had it all figured out, but I was wrong. Dead wrong."

"I've never lied to you. "

"No, you just leave things out." I slammed my phone shut and turned the ringer off. I couldn't take talking to him anymore. I was so desperate that I would eventually start to believe what he said over what was right before my eyes. I didn't want to be the fool who gets taken advantage of. I'd watched it happen in front of my eyes before and I knew how much it hurt.

Chapter 23

"You look like crap." Shauna stood with her hips against my kitchen counter with her arms folded. A position I had come to know meant battle. Once Shauna thought something needed to be done, nothing got in her way. I had once witnessed her convince a six foot ten player to admit he had a drug problem to the coach because she was concerned for his safety. The player was suspended for four months and spent three in a rehab. His admission cost him more than two million dollars in fines.

"Kennedy is not the only man out there. You are beautiful, smart and independent, now start acting like it."

Hearing Kennedy's name made me sad. I had hoped that the last week was a bad dream and that he would come tell me I was wrong and that he loved me, but I hadn't heard from him after our last conversation where I told him I knew he was cheating on me.

I couldn't even cry anymore, I had no more tears after four days of wallowing in my own self pity. "I know you are right, I think I just need some time. It's hard for me to accept the man I love is a cheater. It brings up such bad memories. I saw it with my own eyes, but I still don't want to believe it's true."

"Oh sweetie, I'm so sorry this happened to you, but we need to get you out of here, get some fresh air."

An hour later we were bundled up and walking along 6th Avenue arm in arm. Christmas had hit the city with a vengeance. There were trees and white twinkling lights everywhere. Santas appeared on every street corner shaking a bell while a pot hung patiently waiting for the bustling crowds carrying packages to remember the Christmas spirit. Red velvet ropes with lines of families spread long and wide around department stores offering elaborate holiday themed window displays.

I watched as couples walked hand in hand carrying gifts and packages. A few brave men dragged Christmas trees down the street. It reminded me that I had planned to get a small tree next weekend while Kennedy was in town and have him help me decorate it. But now I didn't want to celebrate or decorate. I just wanted to close my eyes and go back in time and make it all okay again.

I did my best to pretend our long walk did me good, but Shauna could always see right through me. She gave me a hug when we reached my building and made me promise to meet her for drinks Tuesday night.

***

Lauren was startled when she answered the door for Tuesday night dinner. In the fifteen years she had known him, she had never seen Kennedy look anything other than impeccably groomed and confident. "What's wrong? Are you sick? Is Hope okay?"

"I'm fine, Hope and I broke up and I don't want to talk about it." Kennedy hadn't shaved in three days. He wore sweatpants and a thermal, rather than his normal crisp, expensive business suit. His blue eyes were rimmed with dark circles and his normally deep olive skin was sallow.

She glanced at Franklin with concern and gave Kennedy a hug. "I'm sorry honey."

After dinner, Franklin and Kennedy normally sat on the deck for a drink together, but Franklin volunteered to clean up giving Lauren a silent look that she understood. "I'll clean up tonight sweetheart, you had a long week, why don't you go relax and have an after dinner drink with Kennedy and I'll put the kids to sleep."

Outside on the deck was cold in the December air, but Kennedy didn't feel it. Lauren brought Kennedy his usual drink and poured herself an Amaretto to keep warm. "Do I look that bad that he sent in the big guns?" Kennedy took a big gulp from his tumbler and set it down on the end table next to the glider he sat in alone.

Lauren sat across from him rocking in the rocking chair, watching Kennedy's movements. "What happened? I thought you finally found the one?"

Kennedy stared straight ahead. His warm breath visible as he blew out deep into the cold air. "So did I."

"Can it be fixed?"

"She thinks I was with Mikayla. She doesn't trust me."

"Were you?"

Kennedy's head shot to Lauren's face. Daggers in his eyes. "No."

"Did you tell her that?"

He picked up his glass and swallowed back the liquid. "I did, but she doesn't believe me."

"Why wouldn't she believe you? How could she not trust you knowing how you feel about her?

Kennedy winced just slightly, but Lauren caught it. "You didn't tell her how you feel about her, did you?"

Anger tempted his voice. "So it's my fault that she doesn't trust me?"

"I didn't say that. But if she knew what she meant to you, then maybe she would understand that you could never betray her."

Kennedy was silent for a moment. "It's better this way, she was causing me to lose focus on my business."

Lauren rose to her feet. "Kennedy Jenner, I've never known you to be a coward. You take on every challenge you can find and don't give up until you win. But you won't fight for her because you're afraid."

Kennedy stood and stared down at Lauren. "This is bullshit, I don't need this." Then he stormed his way through the house and drove home with his fists clenched around the wheel.

***

The next week passed in a frenzy. The Monet was sold out until long after New Years and the elite of the city held their corporate holiday parties at the hotel. More than 1,000 bold red poinsettias adorned the hotel and small white lights set the backdrop. The hotel looked magical during the holidays, but Hope didn't notice. She worked seven days a week and attended to hundreds of details to make every event perfect.

"Hope, is everything okay with you?" George looked concerned.

"Yes, everything is fine. Did I miss something?" A look of panic on my face.

"No, no, you are doing a great job. I'm not even sure how you are managing it all. But you've seemed so….sad the last two weeks, I thought something was wrong."

I attempted a smile to thank him for his concern. "I'm sorry George, I guess the holidays have me a little down since my boyfriend and I broke up. I didn't mean to let it interfere with my work."

"You're doing a great job. I just wanted to make sure you were okay. Maybe my two left feet could cheer you up if you will save a dance with me at our Christmas party next week."

I smiled. "Sure, why not. That sounds like fun."

***

Saturday night the grand ballroom was filled till 1am with drunken lawyers. The smaller banquet rooms were all filled with parties for three of the larger brokerage houses from downtown. At 2am the lobby of the hotel had turned into a drunken meat market where men in two thousand dollar suits huddled around the last of the women leaving. I said goodnight to the reception staff and made my way to the door in a fog. I was exhausted from all the long hours, and normally would have been more cordial to the man working to get my attention, but I was tired and sad and had no more energy left for men in power suits.

"I'm not interested; please step out of my way."

The tall attractive man was obviously not used to rejection. He put his arm out to touch my waist. "Come on baby; let me buy you a drink."

I kept on walking, ignoring him. But he grabbed my arm in a tight hold. "You fucking bitch."

The doorman saw me approach and walked toward me. "Ms. York, is everything okay?"

I looked at the man who released my arm and then to the doorman. "Yes, I think it is. Thank you, have a good night Ray."

Outside the street was quiet, and I knew I should probably take a taxi, but I had just splurged on a pair of ridiculously expensive boots on one of my 'cheer up Hope' shopping trips with Shauna, and walking was more in my budget than taxis.

A few couples passed by on the street and it pained me to see how happy they looked. Would I ever feel that way again? Two weeks had passed since Kennedy and I broke up, but I still thought about him in every spare moment. As I rounded the corner to make my way across town to my apartment, I was so caught up in my thoughts about Kennedy that I didn't notice the footsteps behind me until I felt a hard tug on my arm.

"You know you want me." The man from the hotel lobby pulled me by my elbow and pinned my arm behind my back. He pulled me close to him. I could smell the liquor on his breath. "You can't ignore me now can you bitch."

I was suddenly aware of his size and anger. The street was desolate. I panicked and pulled my knee up as hard as I could, smashing into his crotch with all my might. He released me and bent over. I watched for a second as he groaned and doubled over. Then I ran, as fast as I could. I was so focused on getting away from him before he righted himself, that I didn't even notice the taxi turning the corner until it was too late.

***

I woke confused and disoriented. My vision was blurry and I had no idea where I was. There were tubes in my arm and a mask over my face and I heard the sounds of beeps coming from all around me. Someone was holding my hand, but I couldn't focus enough to see their face. A woman walked over to me.

"Ms. York, do you know where you are?"

I shook my head.

"You are in the hospital, you were in an accident last night. You were injured, but you are going to be okay. Try to stay still and I'll let the Dr. know you are awake and see if we can remove your mask so you can speak to your husband."

My husband? I turned to the man sitting beside me and worked on bringing the face into focus. Kennedy was staring at me and holding my hand. "It's okay beautiful. You are going to be fine."

I was confused and wasn't quite sure if it was a dream or not. I wanted to focus more but I couldn't keep my eyes open no matter how hard I tried. The doctor must have walked over because I heard him speak.

"Don't be alarmed, I gave her a sedative because she was so upset when she was brought in. She will probably sleep off and on through the night. It looks worse than it is. Her nose is broken and it's normal for her to have two black eyes. There is a lot of swelling so she will probably have some trouble with her vision, but it will improve as the swelling goes down. We had to remove her spleen because of the internal bleeding, so she is going to be sore for a while, but other than that, it looks like she was lucky she didn't suffer any permanent damage."

"Thank you Dr. As soon as she can be moved, I want her in a private room so she can rest."

"I'll let the nurses know, but I would expect she will be in ICU for another day or two for monitoring."

***

I heard my Dad's voice and opened my eyes. He kissed me on the forehead and whispered. "Everything is going to be okay baby girl." I closed my eyes, caught somewhere between sleep and awake.

"Thank you for calling me, Joe." Kennedy still held my hand at my side.

"Of course. Did you just get here?"

"I got here about 6am." Kennedy spoke quietly over me to my dad.

"Oh, I didn't realize you were in the city when I called."

"I wasn't. I chartered a plane and came straight here."

Dad nodded. "How is she?"

"Doctors say she is going to be fine. She was in the operating room when I got here, they had to take out her spleen, but they say it went smoothly and she will make a full recovery." A minute passed and then. "I should have been with her. This is my fault."

"It isn't your fault, son. You are here now, and that's what matters."

***

By the time I woke up it was the middle of the night the day after the accident. Kennedy was still sitting next to me, holding my hand. I watched him sleep for a minute and then his eyes fluttered open as if he sensed I was looking at him.

"Hey beautiful. Can you see better now?" He reached over and removed the mask from my face.

"Yes."

He stood and hovered over me close, looking into my eyes. Then he kissed me gently on the lips. "I'm so sorry Hope."

"Why are you sorry, I'm the one that ran into a taxi?" I tried my best at humor but my throat was dry and sore and the words were barely audible.

Kennedy poured me a glass of water from the pitcher on the tray next to him and held my head up to sip the straw. "Sip"

I did and it burned but felt good.

"I'm sorry I didn't tell you I love you sooner. You didn't believe that I would never cheat on you because I didn't let you know what you meant to me. If I was honest with you, instead of afraid, then you would have understood that I couldn't ever be with another woman again."

Tears stung my eyes and rolled down my cheeks. He gently wiped them away with his thumb. "Please don't cry Hope." He looked into my eyes. "I love you. You are going to be fine. We are going to be fine. I'm not letting it happen any other way."

***

The next morning I was moved to a private room and some of the tubes from my arms were removed. Kennedy had gone to go get some coffee, and I decided it was time I looked in the mirror. I called for the nurse and asked her to help me to the bathroom. An older woman in a nurse's aide uniform came in to help me. We moved slowly and I was a bit dizzy from spending days in bed. But I almost fell when I saw my reflection in the mirror. My face was shades of black and green and my nose was swollen to twice its size. I had to reach out and touch the mirror to make sure it was my own reflection staring back at me.

The nurse's aide saw my face. "It usually looks worse before it gets better, but you are healing nicely. And I wouldn't worry honey, that husband of yours doesn't see what you just saw. He looks at you like you are the only woman in the world. And I'll admit that more than one of the nurses have looked his way, that boy of yours sure is a looker. But he doesn't even notice them. Now he's a keeper. We don't see many of them around here."

I smiled. She put my mind at ease. I tied my robe and steadied myself for the trip back to the bed. As we exited the bathroom, another bed was being rolled into the room. "I thought this was a private room?"

Kennedy walked into the room and came to help me walk with the aide. "It is, but I was tired of sleeping on a chair." He gave me a devilish smile and I rolled my eyes in response playfully.

The Doctor entered the room. "Mr. Jenner made a generous contribution to our clinic and it was the least we could do to thank him. "

***

Being in bed resting all the time had thrown my body's internal clock into a tailspin. Kennedy had set up his laptop in my room to try to keep up with his work, and I noticed he went outside to make phone calls whenever I fell asleep. But for the most part, when I was awake, he was right there next to me.

After the nurse came in to take my vital signs at 2am, I was wide awake and so was Kennedy. He quietly closed the door and gently pulled back the covers and climbed into bed next to me.

I put my head on his chest and listened to his heartbeat. He stroked my hair softly. "Kelly was my high school sweetheart. When we were 15, we had a fight over a cheerleader. Girls had started to notice me and I hadn't learned how to handle the attention yet. I liked it when other girls flirted with me, and I was starting to learn how to flirt back. I think my heart belonged to Kelly, but I was a 15 year old boy with raging hormones and no self control. She took off by herself after our fight and I never saw her again. There were signs of a struggle, and my own investigators watched a suspect for years, but she just vanished."

I felt him struggle to continue. He stopped stroking my hair and wrapped his arm around me tight. "I didn't protect her. It was my fault. I'm not going to let anything happen to you ever again Hope."

My heart broke for the 15 year old boy inside him. I looked up at him in the darkness. "It wasn't your fault. You were 15 and you couldn't have known that something would happen to her after a fight. That's what all kids do. They flirt and fight with their girlfriends. Her disappearing had nothing to do with your fight." I squeezed him hard even though it was painful because of my incision.

He kissed my forehead. "You are the first girl I loved since Kelly. You are the first woman I've ever loved. I don't know how to do this, but I'm going to figure it out. I never wanted anything more in my life."

I looked at him, his face so raw with emotion. "We will figure it out together." Even though I had literally been run over by a car, I had never felt better in my life.

Chapter 24

The next afternoon Charles was waiting out front as Kennedy wheeled me to the hospital exit. "Glad to see you are feeling better Ms. York."

"Thank you Charles"

Kennedy helped me into the back of the car and I looked out the window at the people walking down the sidewalk as we made our way to my apartment. "Do you think the police caught the guy that grabbed me?" We hadn't really discussed the night in detail, although Kennedy was by my side when I gave my statement to the detectives.

I saw his jaw tense. "I think you feel better than he does right now."

My brow creased and I turned to him a little nervous to hear his response. "What does that mean? Were they able to figure out who he was?"

"It's taken care of."

"Did the police arrest him?"

"They arrested him and he made bail the same day. They charged him with assault, but that wasn't enough."

Oh. My. God. "Kennedy, what did you do?"

He moved closer to me and put his arm around me. "You should be more worried about what I am going to do to you when I finally have you alone." His words sent shivers down my spine for more reasons than one.

***

"I really want to take a shower." It felt good to be home and I wanted to wash away the hospital.

Kennedy gave me a devilish grin and started unbuttoning my shirt. When he saw the bandage covering my incision, he reached down and gently kissed all around it. "You aren't supposed to get this wet, so I'll help you."

My face was less black and blue and more yellow and green, but Kennedy didn't seem to notice how horrible I looked. He undressed and we left our clothes in a pile on the floor outside the bathroom. My bathroom shower was small for just me, no less adding six foot two inches of broad man to it. He turned on the water and set the temperature. I stepped in and dropped my head back letting the water run over my hair.

Kennedy stepped inside in front of me and held his hand clasped around my back as I arched into the water. The water felt incredible on my head and my position kept the bandage from being soaked under the water. It also left my entire torso open to Kennedy. His head reached down and gently took my nipple in his mouth. A soft moan escaped. His tongue flicked and licked gently as the water beaded over my head behind me. His gentle licking hardened my nipples and he sucked hard in response to my body's reaction.

I lifted my head from the water stream and he turned me. He removed the shower head from above and carefully directed it to wet my body all over, being careful to keep my bandages dry. He soaped his hands and washed my wet back. His hands were firm and he rubbed as he washed. My body relaxed to his touch. He kissed down the back of my neck and he repositioned the showerhead in his hands to rinse me. He turned me back around and gently eased my legs apart. He positioned the shower head so the water pulsed steady against my clit as he lowered his head to my neck and slowly kissed his way up to my ear.

I whimpered, the water was pulsing hard and desire pulsed through my veins. He bit my nipple and a tremor went through me. The weeks of deprivation from his touch, and days filled with tension, were being released and it was all too much to handle. He positioned the shower head back above and I missed the pulsing stream immediately. I opened my eyes and found him watching me. He put his hands on both sides of my head and pressed his hungry mouth over mine. I was completely under his control. His tongue stroked mine and he sucked on my tongue harshly before breaking the kiss. We both panted loudly.

I gasped at the loss of his mouth and watched as he kneeled in front of me. "Kennedy…." I wasn't sure I could hold myself up to his touch.

"I have you beautiful." He gently positioned my legs spread apart and then his arms tightened around my upper thighs. He positioned his face below my sex as I stood and gently stroked my clit with his tongue. I felt weak, but his arms kept me in place. His tongue drew strong circles around my swollen clit until it was almost too much to bare. I moaned deeply and he flicked and sucked my clit until I came calling his name.

My body felt spineless, and I thought I might lose my balance, but he repositioned me and moved his head further between my legs. Then his tongue was plunging into me deep and hard. I gripped his shoulders and leaned down to deepen the penetration. I came again when he pushed two fingers into me and I looked down. "Good girl. Watch me eat you. I'm going to suck every last sweet drop from you." And he did.

If his hands weren't supporting me, I would have fallen. As he stood up, he reached around the back of my legs and scooped me up, holding me. I could feel his firm cock pushing up against my ass as he carried me to the bed. He gently placed me down in the center of the bed and then hovered over me. His arms on both sides of me bore the brunt of his weight. "I don't want to hurt you, but I need to be inside you."

I reached down and stroked him leisurely, letting him know I wanted him as much as he wanted me. He took my mouth and I felt his hot body lightly against me. I needed him inside of me more than I ever needed anything. I lifted my hips to him and he looked into my eyes as he pushed his long, thick cock inside of me in one strong even stroke.

"God I love how tight you are." His voice was hoarse. He began a firm rhythm in and out, in and out, being careful to keep his weight off of my torso. I rocked my hips up, allowing him to go deeper and he responded with a growl and grinded his hips into me as the root of him pressed firmly against me. His heavy balls slapped hard into my ass as he sunk into me with each forward stroke. I felt him grow harder and then his cock contracted and I felt him fill me. "Fuck."

The uncensored rawness of his pleasure made me gasp and I tumbled over the edge right with him again.

***

I woke the next morning tangled in Kennedy just as I had fallen asleep the night before. I knew he was awake before I raised my eyes to find his. I could feel him watching me intently. "Good morning beautiful." A light kiss on my forehead.

"It's nice waking up to you in my bed instead of the hospital." I snuggled closer wanting to leave no space between us.

"I'll bring your bed to Chicago if you want."

I looked up at him, his eyes were warm and gentle as he gazed at me. "It's not the bed that makes it nice."

"Good, because I like my bed better." He smirked and his playful mood made my heart skip a beat. "So, it's settled then, we'll get rid of your bed and use mine."

"Is that so?"

He kissed me firmly on the lips and nodded once. "Makes sense to me, but if keeping your bed is a deal breaker then I'm good with that too angel."

"But I haven't agreed to move."

"Okay, then let's start with that first, then we can figure out which bed we are keeping." He tried to hide the smile, but the slight indent of a dimple gave him away.

"Kennedy, I...."

He put his finger over my mouth. "I fucked up Hope. I should never had taken no for an answer the first time I asked you to move in with me. I'm not taking no for an answer now, so you might as well understand that before you make your decision." His pale blue eyes searched mine, holding me where he wanted me. "Chicago is where my business is, so it's difficult for me to live anywhere else. But if you are not ready to move, I'll move to New York. I'll figure it out.

I'll buy this building and move in one of the apartments here if that's what you want. But, you have to know, unless you tell me you don't love me anymore, I'm going to be where you are, wherever that is."

I knew deep down in my heart that I loved this incredible, sexy, bossy man. I looked into his eyes. I remembered being a little girl and watching my dad look at my mom, I couldn't describe what it was, but I knew that he loved her more than anything in the world. I'd never seen a man look at a woman that way. Until today. I made my decision in that moment and he must have seen it happen on my face. He smiled at me. The glorious full dimple smile.

"Okay." It came out as a whisper.

"Okay?" He sounded as if it was a surprise, but we both knew it wasn't.

I rolled my eyes playfully. "I'll move to Chicago."

He pressed his lips softly to mine. "Thank you beautiful. I love you."

***

A week went by and Kennedy was true to his word. He didn't let me out if his sight. He took me for all of my follow up doctor's appointments, and sat and held my hand when my stitches were removed. My kitchen table was converted into Jenner Holdings command central, and he worked while I rested and slowly started to pack. I called George and told him I was going to be leaving the first week in January, after the Christmas and New Year's events were behind us. He said he was sad I was leaving, but he understood and was happy for me.

"I hate the thought of you going back to work tomorrow angel." His voice was stern.

"We already had this discussion Kennedy. I can't leave them during the busiest two weeks of the year. I need to go back tomorrow to help. It's the least that I can do considering I am leaving after only three months."

"I'm putting a bodyguard on you when you are not with me. He'll stay out of your way, but he won't be more than a hundred feet away."

A streak of heat moved through my body, as it always did when Kennedy took that powerful commanding tone. "It's not necessary, but if it will make you feel better."

"It will."

I smiled, having learned which battles were worth fighting with Kennedy, this one didn't make the list. "Okay honey."

I squeezed my body in between the table and Kennedy and sat myself on his lap, straddling him. My hands rested on his shoulder and he pulled me closer to him, pressing himself into me.

"I was thinking. Maybe we should take your brother to a game while he is in town. Shauna can get us tickets and we could grab a bite after it's over."

One eyebrow arched. "You are not trying to play matchmaker are you?"

"No." I lied.

Kennedy looked at me suspiciously. "Ok, set it up. He arrives this Thursday night and he's staying till Sunday."

"I already checked, they are playing at home on Friday night. So we can do it then." I gave a victorious smile.

"Don't smile at me with that cute smile. Or my next video conference will be watching your ass go up and down on this chair in about three minutes."

I felt my face pink and I pictured him naked and glistening with sweat as I held his thick shoulders and rode the length of him up and down in full, long strokes.

He watched me, his gaze fixed on my mouth. "Fuck, Hope." Then he dialed his secretary and told her to push his conference back and hour. I squirmed on top of him as he spoke. Then I rode him until we were both exhausted and took a nap naked on the couch where he could watch me while he worked the rest of the afternoon.

Chapter 25

Garrett acted every bit the eligible bachelor as the Chicago papers had made him out to be. I had started to get used to the way women looked at Kennedy, with their mouths watering and perky breasts thrust forward. It didn't bother me because Kennedy never reacted to it. His focus was always on me, and I was never quite sure if he ignored the looks he got for my benefit or if he had just grown immune to them. Garrett, on the other hand, took full advantage of every opportunity that came his way.

Shauna had landed us court side tickets and I was excited to show off my best friend. I was pretty sure the VIP waitress was neglecting the other patrons when she spent ten minutes flirting with Garrett on her fourth trip over to make sure we didn't need anything else. As the cheerleaders made their way onto the floor for their half time show, I decided I was done with the sexy server.

"Garrett, Shauna is the third one from the right." I motioned to the right side of the kick line forming. Garrett took one look at Shauna and forgot the waitress was standing there waiting for his attention.

"We are good for now." I smiled at the waitress dismissively and she huffed away.

Garrett followed Shauna with his eyes. She smiled and winked at us as she moved into position for her squad's performance.

"Did I tell you that you were my favorite brother?" Garrett leaned towards Kennedy without taking his eyes off Shauna.

I smiled up at Kennedy and pretended to be surprised by Garrett's reaction, but Kennedy knew better. He shook his head at me and gave me a look that said I might be in trouble later.

***

After the game was over we went to a bar that Garrett picked. The beautiful hostess was excited to see Garrett and sized up Shauna with disapproval as she led us to a VIP section that overlooked a dance floor below. Shauna had changed out of her uniform and into jeans with strategically placed rips and knee high black leather boots. She wore a tight black t-shirt emblazoned with the team name in crystals across her chest. Her wrists were covered with sparkly silver and crystal bracelets; she looked like naughty Barbie, a figment of every man's wet dream.

Kennedy and Garrett went to the bar to grab our drinks and Shauna told me how gorgeous she thought Garrett was.

Two guys stopped by the table "Can we buy you ladies a drink?" the shorter one with the hulking muscles asked.

I looked at Shauna and then back at the guys, who clearly were not used to rejection with the way that they looked standing there gorgeous and confident. I was about to decline, and explain that we were there with people, when I felt Kennedy's presence behind me.

"Move along." Kennedy said with a steel face and dismissive hand gesture.

Kennedy settled in on the seat beside me, his arm draped behind me in a possessive stance. I caught Shauna's eye and she gave me an approving smile.

"Let's go Garrett. I can read a lot about a man on the dance floor and I'm wondering what kind of book you are." Shauna arched one eyebrow mischievously and Garrett grabbed her hand and led her down to the dance floor.

We watched as they danced and quickly found their rhythm together. My gaze slid over Kennedy. He wore steel grey dress pants and a dark grey cashmere v neck sweater. His normally pale blue eyes picked up the color of his clothes and changed the color to an unusual grey blue. He looked urbane and ridiculously sexy. I could never get used to how gorgeous this man is.

"You're doing it again." His voice was low and gruff.

I snapped out of my momentary visual admiration of him. Confused. "Doing what?"

"Looking at me like an angel that I want to take home and fuck till the devil comes out."

Shocked by his words, I gasped, crossing my legs together tightly to reign in my body's reaction to his strength. "Oh boy."

He blew out a loud breath and set down his drink. He turned to me. "I'm killing myself trying to push down the urge to beat the shit out of a man who tried to buy you a drink and you are sitting there looking at me like I'm a gift you want to unwrap. You have no fucking clue. What did I ever do to deserve you Hope?"

I studied his face, taking in every detail. "You made me believe who I am."

His lips covered mine and he kissed me. For a minute there was nothing but Kennedy and me. The music disappeared and all of the people around us. When he released me, I whispered in his ear. "I love you." He smiled then reached in to whisper in my ear. "I love you too beautiful."

Shauna and Garrett spent a long time dancing and I was thrilled that they liked each other as much as I had hoped. When Shauna tried to get me to dance with her, I felt Kennedy go stiff and I knew it was more than he could handle tonight. Kennedy announced it was time to call it a night, and Charles appeared out front when we finally made our way through the crowds.

"Ummm, we will take a rain check on the ride big brother, I'm going to walk Shauna home." Garrett was holding Shauna's hand and she beamed at me and winked and blew me a kiss. Kennedy and I climbed in to the limo.

"Where to Mr. Jenner?" Charles asked.

"Home." Kennedy responded and I realized it didn't matter where we lived, I was home wherever I was with him.

***

My first week back to work flew by and I barely had time to notice the hulk like man that Kennedy had hired to watch over me. Christmas was on Sunday and I was excited that we had a three day weekend, even though I had only just returned to work. We had decided to go to Chicago for the weekend and spend Christmas with his brother and his family. After my last day at my job, we would go to Oregon for a week and have a late Christmas with my Dad. I knew Dad was worried when he left after my accident, but I also knew that Kennedy had been calling him and giving him updates ever since he went back home.

Chapter 26

When we arrived at Kennedy's apartment on Christmas Eve, I was elated to find a twelve foot tall Christmas tree gleaming with thousands of twinkling lights. It was decorated entirely in silver and red and it looked as if it had just been torn from a layout in Good Housekeeping magazine.

"When did you find the time to do all this?" Kennedy walked up behind me and wrapped his arms around me.

"I had a decorator come and get the house ready for us."

The apartment was dark, except for the lights from the sparkling tree. It looked magical. "It's beautiful, thank you."

"I'm glad you like it, it's the first tree I've ever had of my own."

My voice gave away my shock. "What? You never had a Christmas tree before?"

"Nope. I go to Franklin's every year for Christmas, so I never saw the point of putting one up."

"But we are going to Franklin's for Christmas this year too?"

Kennedy thought for a minute. "I guess I never had anything to celebrate before."

I reached up on my tippy toes and kissed him gently on the mouth. "We both have something to celebrate this year."

***

I woke up on Christmas morning before Kennedy, which was rare. I watched him sleep for a while, in awe of his chiseled jaw and perfect lips. I couldn't imagine a day when looking at him didn't take my breath away. He was just so perfectly masculine. Even sleeping he exuded a raw sexuality. It took more than a little self control to not wake him, but we both had a rough couple of weeks, and he needed his sleep.

I went to the kitchen and made coffee. I stared at the majestic tree in the dark for a while and reflected on Kennedy's words from the night before. Beneath that strong, dark exterior was a beautiful thoughtful man. A man that loved me. A man that wanted to live with me. The thought made me warm inside.

I caught a glimpse of Kennedy out of the corner of my eye as I was spooning the eggs onto plates. He stood in the doorway, leaning into the doorjamb casually with his arms crossed. His body filled the doorway and his face looked amused.

"That smells good. But I would have liked to have had breakfast in bed." He smirked.

"I was working on it, but you came out before the bacon was done." I pouted.

"I wasn't talking about bacon and eggs." His smile was sinful.

I could feel my face flush and his stare was unwavering. "Oh."

"I have a Christmas gift to give you." He took two long strides and reached out and pulled me into his arms.

I looked up at him and felt the heat in my face ignite. "I bet you do."

He laughed and his pale eyes brightened. His sexy smile made me tingle and I wrapped my arms around him.

"You look so fucking sexy wearing that t-shirt and standing in the kitchen making breakfast. I had a hard on before I even touched you." He pressed his hips into me to validate his words.

"Behave," I admonished. "Our breakfast is going to get cold and I want to give you your present before we go to Franklin's house."

"I'll behave if you promise I can fuck you bent over your desk at your new job very soon." His voice was low and sultry.

"Isn't that a little premature? I haven't even started yet!"

"Just promise me that if the opportunity presents itself, you'll be ready for me. I've been dreaming about it for days."

I was aroused just thinking about what he said, and he knew it. His smile was devious and delicious.

I breathed out an exaggerated sigh as if I was doing him a big favor. "Okay, fine, *if* the opportunity presents itself."

***

We ate breakfast and exchanged gifts. I hadn't had much time to for shopping, but Shauna had helped me pick up a few things that I knew I wanted to get him. It was no surprise to me that Kennedy had overdone it. For my first gift, he led me into the bedroom and opened a closet door. He had emptied a whole closet for me and it was already filled with clothes and shoes. Rows of beautiful designer clothing lined the walls and I was sure he had made some personal shopper a very fat Christmas commission.

As if all of his generousness wasn't enough. "I have one more gift for you. But you need to get dressed to see it."

"Kennedy, you are insane. You've already bought me too much!"

"Don't worry beautiful, this one is as much for me as it is for you." He smacked my ass. "Now go cover up that sweet little ass, so I can take you out in public."

As usual, I dutifully complied with his command. Kennedy wouldn't tell me where we were going. We pulled up in front of a beautiful hotel and Kennedy came around and opened my door.

"Good morning, Mr. Jenner." The valet said as he caught the keys that Kennedy threw his way.

We made our way to the second floor when the hotel manager caught up to us. "Mr. Jenner, how nice to see you. Everything that you requested is in order."

"Good. I won't be needing anything else today." Our pace quickened with his blatant dismissal of the manager who looked a bit disappointed.

We arrived at the door that Kennedy was looking for, and he handed me a set of keys. I noticed that the keychain had a script J on it and the plaque on the door read *Hope York*. He smiled and motioned with his hand for me to step forward to unlock the door.

Inside was an elegantly decorated office. It was professional, with a touch of whimsy. A large antique desk with carved legs sat in the middle of the office. In one corner was a picture of Kennedy and I taken the night of the Kelly's charity dinner, and we were both smiling and looking at each other. In the other corner was a crystal business card holder. I picked up one of the cards, *Hope York, Event Manager.* On the opposite side of the desk sat three different, uniquely upholstered Queen Anne style chairs. In the corner was a large lithographic of the ice cream painting that hung in our bedrooms.

I felt my eyes sting as I took it all in. "How did you do all this?" The tears rolled down my face as I looked at him and saw him watching me closely, wanting my approval.

"Fuck angel, don't cry."

I sniffled unattractively through my tears. "I love you."

He lifted my chin forcing me to look at him. "I love you too angel, Merry Christmas."

He lowered his mouth to mine and covered my lips with his in a gentle kiss. He leaned his forehead against mine. His pale eyes turned dark with lust. "Looks like the opportunity has presented itself."

There was no way that I would be able to say no to him. He had done so much to make me feel at home, and had been so generous to me. I wanted to show him how much I appreciated all that he had done. Besides, the man was simply irresistible.

He crossed the room quickly and locked the door, then slid behind me in front of my new desk. Then I let him do just as I promised...fuck me bent over my new desk.

***

Franklin and Lauren's house was filled with the electricity of an excited child on Christmas morning. Emily had convinced Lauren to let her open one of our gifts, and I was thrilled with how excited she was when she opened her new Easy Bake Oven. It was my favorite toy when I was a little girl, and I had hoped that she didn't already have one.

Emily and I were busy making a mini chocolate cake in her new oven when I heard the doorbell and Garrett's voice. I heard some introductions and murmuring, but Emily and I were too focused on watching the light bulb cook the little cake to notice anyone walk into the room.

"Well is this what you are going to do in Chicago all day, bake little mini cakes and play house?" There was no mistaking that voice. I turned.

"Shauna! What are you doing here?" I ran and hugged her and we stayed that way for a minute.

"Garrett and I wanted to see each other again and Kennedy thought it would be a nice surprise for me to come visit you!" We giggled like two school girls who just landed the captain of the football team.

I looked up and saw Kennedy watching us intently. He gave me the full blown dimple smile and I mouthed *I love you*.

Shauna quickly bonded with Lauren and the three of us spent half the day drinking wine and taking turns telling stories about Shauna and me in high school and Garrett and Kennedy in high school. We giggled like old friends, and every once in a while I looked across the room and saw Kennedy watching me with a smile. I could tell he was enjoying his time with his brothers, but yet he was always aware of where I was.

"Hey!" I called out when I saw him standing leaning against the kitchen counter with his arms crossed staring at me, while his brothers were in the midst of a conversation next to him. "What are you looking at?" I smiled and he smiled back.

Kennedy refilled his glass and reached for the half empty bottle of wine the three of us were drinking and walked over to where we were standing. He refilled each of our glasses. Shauna and Lauren mindlessly positioned their glasses for refills, while never breaking in their conversation. He slid behind me and wrapped his arms tightly around mine, clasping my hands together beneath his.

Shauna was telling Lauren a story that I had heard a dozen times, about the time that we cut school and took her dad's car to the beach to meet two boys. One of the boys had brought iced tea spiked with vodka and Shauna had drunk too much and I had to drive home. The only problem was that I had never driven a stick shift car, and it took us almost three hours to drive the twenty miles drive home between all of my stalls and clutch pops. Two blocks from her house, I rear ended the car in front of us, which happened to be the two boys that we had met at the beach. In the three hours it took us to get home, they had already sobered up and drove back.

"I hope you don't drive a stick shift Kennedy." Shauna laughed as she finished her story.

"No, and I'll keep that in mind when we go new car shopping for her next week."

"New car shopping?" I wrinkled my nose in confusion at him.

I watched him take his drink off the mantle and swallow back the yellow liquid in the small crystal tumbler. His other hand stayed on my hip. "How did you think you were going to get around Chicago? We don't have the mass transportation that New York has, you need a car here."

"Ugh...I hadn't really thought about it. How far is it? Can't I walk to work? I really can't afford a car payment."

"*We* can afford a car angel. And you are *not* walking to work no matter how far it is. Look what happened last time you walked home after a late night."

My chest fluttered at his commanding tone and the thought of us being a *we*. But I couldn't let him buy me a car, even if he was ridiculously rich. "That's very sweet, but it isn't your job to take care of me."

Well that was the wrong thing to say. His eyes hardened and his jaw tensed immediately. Our playful, giggly conversation had just turned into something else. "It is my job and perhaps we should have this conversation later."

I saw Shauna and Lauren watching our interaction as if we were a daytime soap opera. Lauren was smiling at me and I got the feeling she thought the whole conversation was funny for some reason. Not wanting to ruin the day or show any disrespect to Lauren in her home, I took a deep breath and decided Kennedy was right, and the conversation was best for when we were in private later. I smiled back at Lauren and turned to Kennedy and reached up on my tippy toes and gave him a quick kiss on the mouth. "Okay, later it is."

He must have assumed I would react differently, because he squinted at me and smiled, shaking his head as he walked back to his brothers.

Lauren excused herself and Shauna and I were finally alone. "What's going on with you and Garret?" My smile widened.

Shauna launched into details about the long night they spent together after we had all went to her game and then out to the bar. I could have skipped the part about how he had what she estimated to be about ten inches hidden in his pants. But I secretly wasn't surprised knowing that Kennedy was his brother. She told me that they had been texting and talking every day since, which caught me by surprise. "You talk to him every day?" The look of shock clearly registering on my face.

"Yep, I can't believe it myself. This is the most I have spoken to a guy in a long time without him breaking any of my top ten rules. I'm so excited that I think I'm going to reward him later dressed in my modified cheer uniform."

We both laughed. Shauna hated when men mentioned that she should wear her cheer uniform as foreplay. But if she really liked them, and they didn't mention it, she would introduce them to her 'modified cheer uniform', which meant an old skirt that left her ass cheeks hanging out and a low cut tight cheer top, sans bra and underwear.

"I'm so sad that I am not going to be near you in the city anymore, if you guys became a couple you could move to Chicago and be closer to me!" The alcohol and my current state of happy daze had made things seem so simple and easy to solve.

Shauna looked at me like I was crazy and then broke down laughing. "You are so funny drunk and in love. I used to love drunk Hope, but I think drunk in love Hope is even better!"

***

It was after midnight by the time we returned back to Kennedy's apartment, and I felt like I was floating. Kennedy poured me a glass of wine and I watched him build a fire. I could see the muscles in his back flex as he reached in to pile the wood and I was sure that there wasn't one part of him that I didn't find sexy. We sat on the floor in front of the fire with only the Christmas tree and fire lit.

"Thank you for the best Christmas I ever had." I whispered as I settled in between his propped up knees in front of the fire.

He kissed my forehead lightly. "You're welcome, but I didn't do anything. Garret and Lauren did all the work."

Was he serious? "You cleaned out a closet, bought me a new wardrobe, gave me a new job with an amazing memory in my new office and brought my best friend to Chicago."

"Those have nothing to do with Christmas. I would have done all of that if it was August and you agreed to move here." He gently stroked my hair, pushing escaped tendrils behind my ear and a soothing motion. "So now that I think about it, I really didn't give you a Christmas present."

The man was crazy. "Your logic is a little warped there Mr. Jenner." I laughed and tilted my head into his touch on the side of my face.

"As long as we are on the topic of my logic, I'm buying you a car. We can call it your Christmas present if that makes you feel any better." His voice was stern.

"I can't let you buy me a car too Kennedy." I turned and leaned into him. "It's very sweet of you to want to, but it's too much."

He contemplated my words with narrowed eyes. "What I have is yours now, Hope. I live a certain way. I work hard for it, and I enjoy my lifestyle and a certain amount of indulgence. We can't exist in two different worlds. I want to take care of you. I need to take care of you. Let me."

With just his few simple words and the look in his eyes, I realized it was important to him. He needed to take care of me. He didn't just want me, he needed me. I understood what he meant. "Okay." I whispered lightly, his eyes not releasing mine.

Chapter 27

I was a nervous wreck on the drive to Dad's house from the airport, because I hadn't told Dad I was moving to Chicago yet. Moving in with Kennedy.

"You okay?" He squeezed the hand he was holding as I stared out the window watching the city fall into the distance and the small town on the horizon.

"Yes, just tired." I lied.

"Hope." His tone was authoritative and I wondered how he knew I was lying so instinctively.

I leaned my head against the cold window glass as my face flushed giving away my lie. "I might also be a little nervous about telling my Dad that I'm moving in with you."

He pulled our linked hands to his mouth and gently kissed the back of my hand. "I'll talk to him about it."

"You will?" Even though I was 26 years old, I still felt like a little girl when I was around my dad.

"Of course I will. I should have probably spoken to him about it before now anyway."

***

Candace did her usual gushing over Kennedy and touched me as little as possible while pretending to be happy to see me too. I left Kennedy in the attentive hands of Candace and her awe struck daughters and went to settle in and put our things away. A few hours later, my Dad still wasn't home yet, so I thought it would a perfect time to go visit Mom. I hadn't been able to spend more than an hour or two in the house with Candace without Dad home in years. There was only so much that I could take of her, and watching her flirt with Kennedy was pushing me to my limit.

"I need to get out of here for a while." I whispered to Kennedy quietly. He nodded.

"Candace, we are going to go over to the cemetery, we will be back in a few hours." I saw her jaw flex and anger flicker from her eyes and wondered if Kennedy saw it too. The man didn't even have to look at me to know if I was lying, I was certain he would be able to see through Candace's fake exterior.

We stopped at the florist and I picked out flowers for Mom and Kennedy picked out flowers for Lilly. As we were about to walk out of the shop, I walked straight into Coach Fitz. There was no way to avoid him. "Umm…Hi Coach Fitzsimmons." I uttered and a sudden awkward feeling settled in.

"Hello Hope. Nice to see you." The awkwardness between us was thick. He looked to Kennedy and Kennedy extended his hand.

"Kennedy Jenner." They shook hands.

"Mark Fitzsimmons." An uncomfortable silence for a moment. "Umm..I was a Coach at Hope's high school."

I felt flush and wanted to run out of the store. Kennedy looked to me and then to the Coach, assessing the situation.

"Is that so." His face was a mask of stone and his tone icy. Kennedy put his hand on the small of my back and steered me around Coach and out the door.

Neither of us said a word the short drive to the cemetery. I was glad that he suggested we drive, because the walk in the cold would have been frigid with the ice between us. We cleared off the ground in front of Mom and Lilly's headstones in uncomfortable silence and rested the flowers on the brown frozen grass.

Kennedy sat on the bench, watching me as I fidgeted with the flowers, stalling for time before I had to face him. "You and Coach have a past." More of a statement than a question.

I continued to clean the brown grass and pick at imaginary weeds. "Yes, but it's not what you are thinking."

He reached out and took my hand and let out a deep breath. "Jealousy is not something that I am used to feeling. I know you must have had boyfriends, but I saw the tension between you and him and I wanted to beat the crap out of him. I had to get out of there."

Tears stung my eyes and I closed my eyes and squeezed his hand. I knew I had to tell him the truth. No lies, not ever. "You should have beat the crap out of him." He looked up at me and I saw pain in his face. "It's a long story. Could we go for a walk while I tell you, it's not something I'd like to tell you here."

He nodded and took my hand. We walked through the cemetery, and around town, for almost two hours in the cold. I told him the whole sordid story, from Candace's affair to the years of living with a stepmother that hated me and pretending everything was okay for Dad. I told him how she blamed me for Dad finding out and the ensuing difficulty in their relationship. I watched his jaw tighten as I told him through tears that, after so many years, I started to believe the things that she said, and that my move to New York was to get away and reinvent myself.

He wiped the tears from my face and cupped my cheeks. "She was jealous of you."

"Why would Candace ever be jealous of me?" Shauna had said the same thing a few times before, but I thought she was just trying to make me feel better.

"Jesus Hope, you really have no clue." His face was serious as he searched my eyes. "You are beautiful, from head to toe. And not just on the outside. The fact that you don't see it or use it just makes you that much more gorgeous." He kissed my lips gently. "She's an aging beauty queen that is desperate for attention and you don't even notice all the attention you get."

My heart swelled at his words. I wanted so badly to believe him. To see myself the way he saw me. I was so afraid to admit who I was to him, but he didn't see me any different after knowing. I loved him for understanding me and for giving me back a part of who I used to be.

***

Dad was in good mood all night and really seemed to enjoy sitting with Kennedy. It was odd seeing him relaxing with a man that wasn't his friend. He was always surrounded by girls. Me, mom, the twins, Candace. I found myself wondering if maybe dad regretted never having a son. Maybe him and mom would have tried for a boy if she hadn't died so young. He and Kennedy laughed like old friends, and it warmed my heart to see the two men that I loved getting along so well. I noticed that Kennedy seemed to appear whenever I was alone with Candace, and I wasn't sure if it was a coincidence or he was being protective.

Candace had drunk an entire bottle of wine herself, and I could tell it was bringing out a mean streak. We were just finishing cleaning up after dinner in the kitchen when her claws came out. "Your father tells me you are moving in with Kennedy. You know, men don't like women that make it that easy for them." She slurred her words and tilted her head back to empty her glass. "I guess it shouldn't surprise me that you have no idea how to keep a man's interest."

I felt my face burning with anger as I continued to put away the last of the dishes.

From behind me, his calm and cool tone, sent shivers up my spine. "Hope has more than my interest." I turned and could tell he was keeping his voice down so that Dad wouldn't hear.

His appearance had Candace flustered, but she was a pro at masking the evil within. "I was just telling our little Hope that sometimes men don't buy the cow, when they get the milk for free." She trailed her perfectly manicured finger flirtatiously across Kennedy's back as she passed him on her way out of the kitchen. Watching her touch him made me sick to my stomach. I watched as his whole body tensed at her touch.

I walked to him and put my hands flat on his chest, leaning into him. "You okay?" he asked as he ran his hands up and down my back.

I did my best attempt at a smile. "I'm not going to let her get to me." I lied. Honestly, the woman knew how to zone in on my biggest fears. Would he get bored of me? He was gorgeous and worldly and rich. Men like him didn't belong with boring small town girls like me.

He squinted at me, as if he wasn't sure I was telling the truth. "Really, I'm fine. Let's go back to Dad before he realizes that anything is wrong."

He squeezed me and led me to the living room. I wasn't sure he believed me, but he was giving me a free pass.

Dad had made Candace and the twins keep one present unopened from Christmas, so that we could all open gifts together, since I hadn't exchanged with them yet. Dad and I were giving out gifts to everyone when I noticed Candace take a seat on the small loveseat next to Kennedy. It was a small loveseat, so normally people had to sit close, but Candace looked like she was sitting extra close. When I looked at Kennedy I could see his jaw was tight and he had noticed it too.

I walked over to Candace and held out a gift to her without saying a word. She smiled a sugar coated plastic smile up at me and snatched it out of my hands. I made a point of ignoring her and turned my face to Kennedy and handed him a gift.

"You already gave me gifts." His voice was calm, but I knew he was controlling anger sitting so close to Candace.

"I saved one to open here." I smiled at him and watched as his face untensed.

He gave me a little smile back. "I saved one for you too." One eyebrow arched and my knees quivered at his naughty dimpled smile. I felt my face flush

Candace made a loud fake cough, bringing us back to the room. I opened my eyes wide to Kennedy in a silent, playful "stop it" face and walked back to Dad.

I opened one of the gifts dad had given me. It was a pretty keychain with a large dangling silver star.

"Thanks Dad, it's very pretty."

"I don't care if it's pretty baby girl, it's got a secret alarm built in." He took the keychain and pressed the sides of the bottom and it emitted a high pitched, ear piercing, loud alarm sound.

I smiled and laughed. "Thanks Dad, I'll use it. But I told you I am fine."

He kissed my forehead. "I know you are, I trust Kennedy to take good care of you."

You do? My dad trusts Kennedy to take good care of me? When did that happen?

"I'm sure you will be alone an awful lot living out there in Chicago. I mean Kennedy is a busy business man and I'm sure he has a lot of functions and travel that monopolizes his time. Your daddy and I just want to make sure you are safe, Hope." Candace's words came out an odd mixture of slur and sugary.

"Actually, I don't plan on going to any functions or traveling anywhere without Hope, now that she is moving to Chicago." Kennedy didn't look at Candace as he spoke.

"That's what you say now, but things can change."

"Candace." The whole room went quiet at his one word. His tone said it all.

But Candace never knew when to stop. "Well someone has to look out for our little Hope. I'm just afraid that she will wind up all alone while Kennedy is busy in his world." The words sounded inconspicuous, but I knew what she meant. We were from different worlds and I didn't belong in his.

"They will be fine. And I don't think this is the time or place to discuss any concerns you might have." My Dad rarely raised his voice, but his curt response was loud and clear.

Kennedy stood and I was afraid that he had reached his limit and had enough. I knew he was protective of me; I walked toward him needing to touch him to keep him calm.

"That's okay, Joe. I'd like to put Candace's mind at ease, so that she isn't concerned." Kennedy reached out and took my hand and brought it to his lips, kissing the top of my hand gently. He looked me in the eyes. "Candace doesn't have to worry about me being busy in my world without you, because you are my world." He paused but his eyes never looked away from mine. "I don't have any functions anymore, *we* have functions." I watched as he looked to Dad and Dad gave him a smile and head nod. Then he turned back to me. "But there is one thing Candace is right about, things can change. And I hope they will, really soon." He looked down and reached into his pocket. "I've been carrying this around in my pocket since the night you were in the accident. It was my mother's ring. But tonight I asked Joe for his blessing, and he thought you should have this one instead." He fished into his pocket again and I saw my mother's ring. My eyes filled with tears. Shock. Excitement. Love. Happiness. I wanted to scream and jump up and down, but I was frozen.

His large hand gently cupped my chin and tilted it up to meet his gaze. "Hope Marie York, I know I'm not good enough for you, but will you let me spend the rest of my life in your world?"

My head started to spin and I realized I had been holding my breath. Kennedy leaned down, his head next to mine, he whispered. "Breathe angel, breathe."

I exhaled and the tears started flowing uncontrollably.

He wiped my tears away. "Give me an answer beautiful."

"Yes." I whispered.

"Yes?" He whispered back and smiled down at me.

"Yes!" I yelled. "Yes, Yes, I want to marry you!" I wrapped my arms around him and hugged him tight. He smiled and looked down at me.

"Welcome to the family son." Dad patted Kennedy on the back. I hugged Dad.

"Thank you Dad." I whispered as I hugged him. Over Dad's shoulder I saw Candace's face and could barely hold back hysterical laughter. Her mouth was hanging open and she was pale, as if she had just seen a ghost.

***

By the time we went to bed that night, I felt as though I was floating. I was happier than I ever thought possible. I was going to marry the man of my dreams, who loved me and would protect me with his life. I stared at my mother's beautiful ring as Kennedy climbed into bed next to me.

"I love you." I said softly.

"I love you too beautiful." His mouth covered mine for a soft kiss.

He lifted his head to look me in the eyes as he moved his body over mine, resting his weight on his arms. I felt the stiffness between his legs brush my leg as he shifted his body to settle between my legs. "Now I'm going to give you the present I have been saving for you." I saw the corners of his dirty smile and caught a glimpse of his dimples as he reached up and turned off the light. And then he gave me another present.

Printed in Great Britain
by Amazon